MENAGERIE 4

ADULT ANTHROPOMORPHIC FOLIO

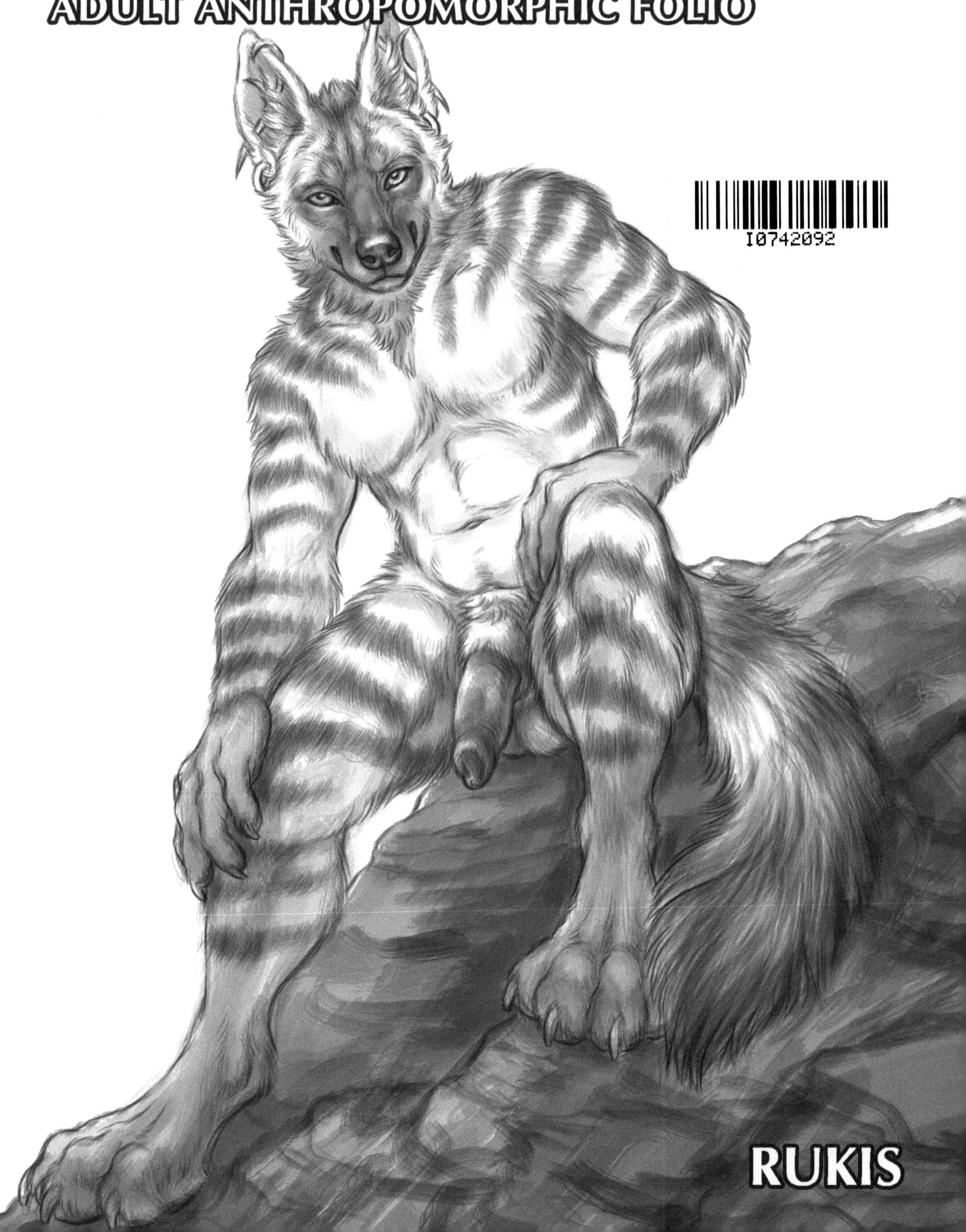

RUKIS

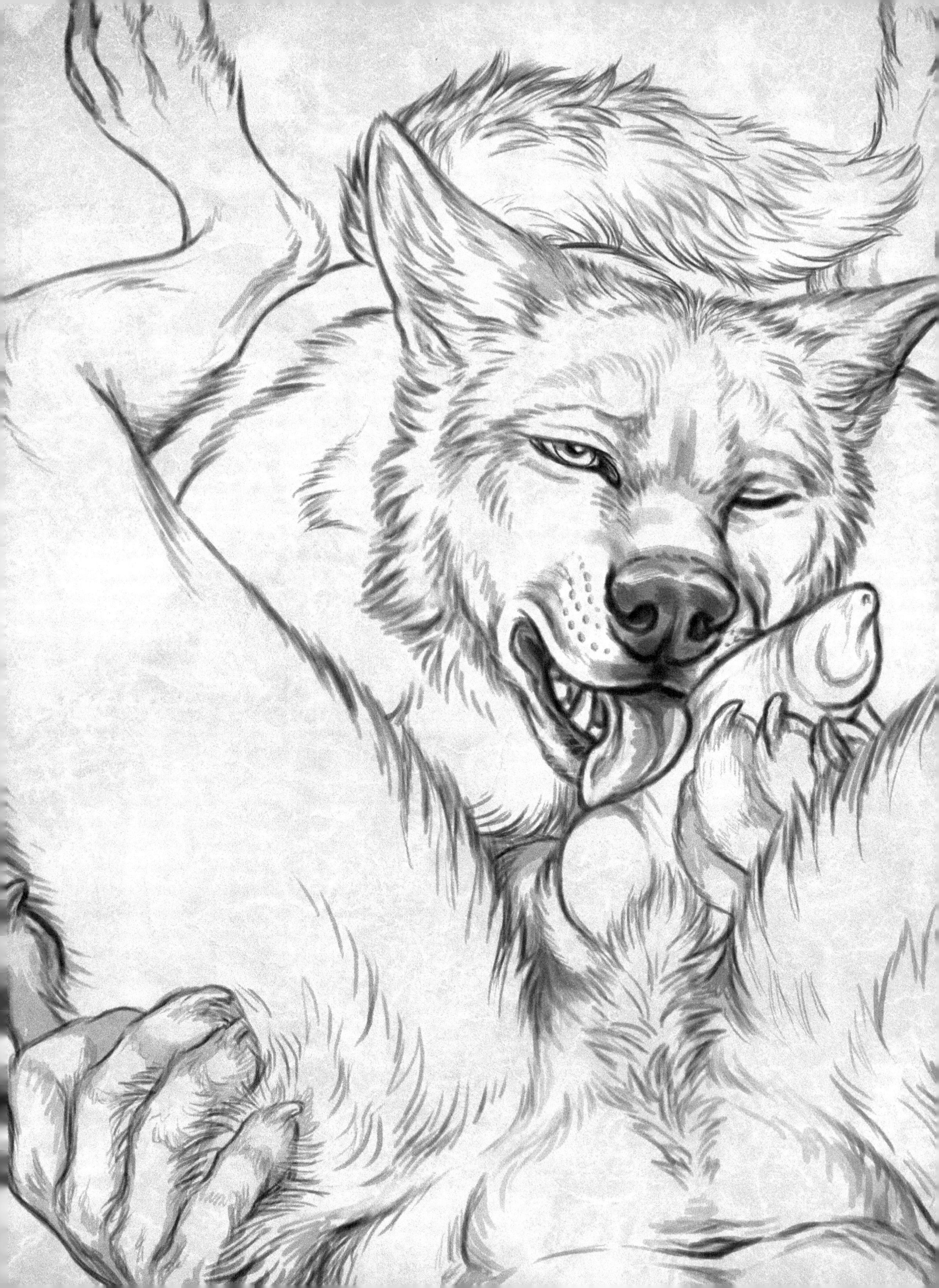

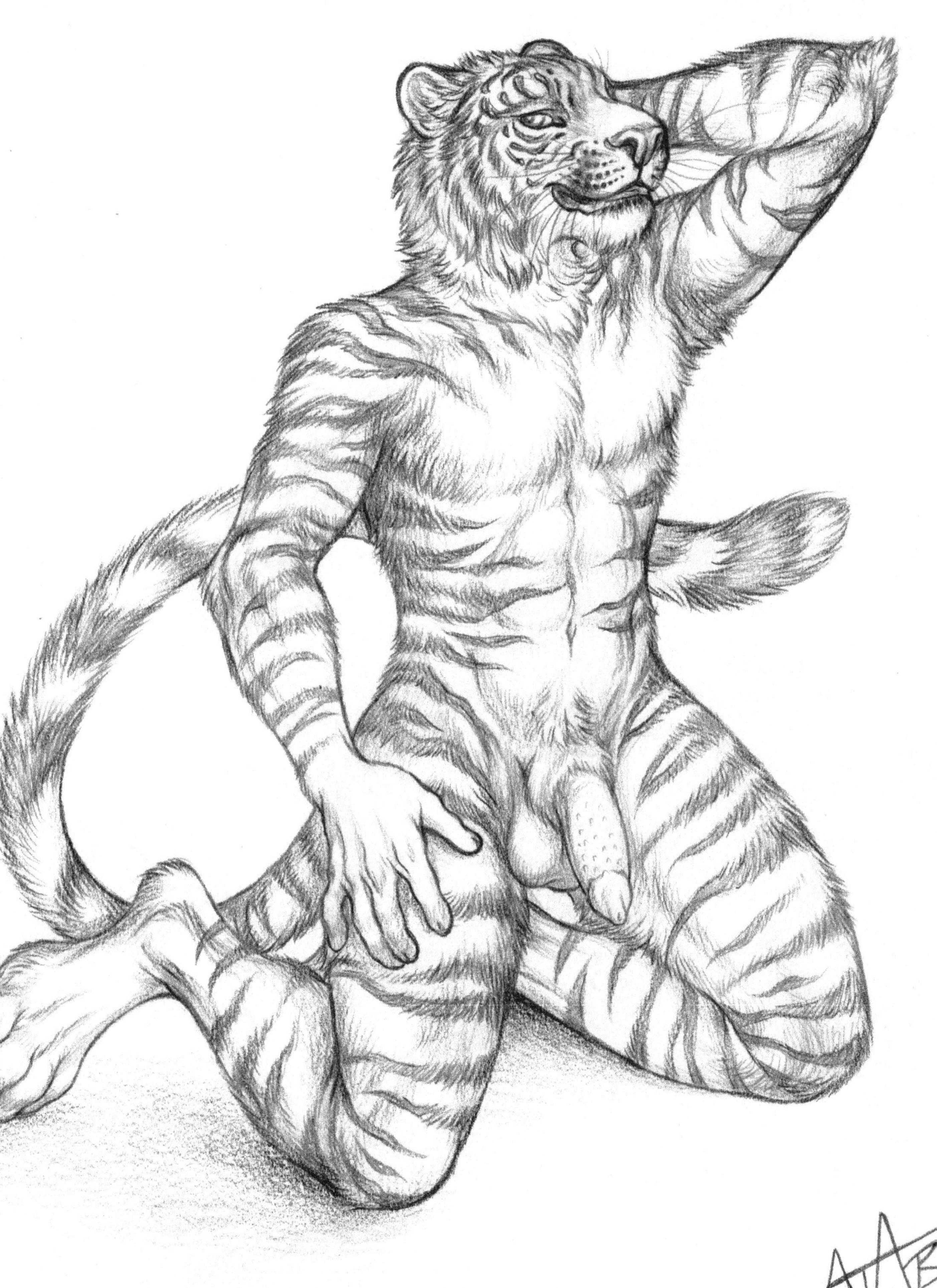

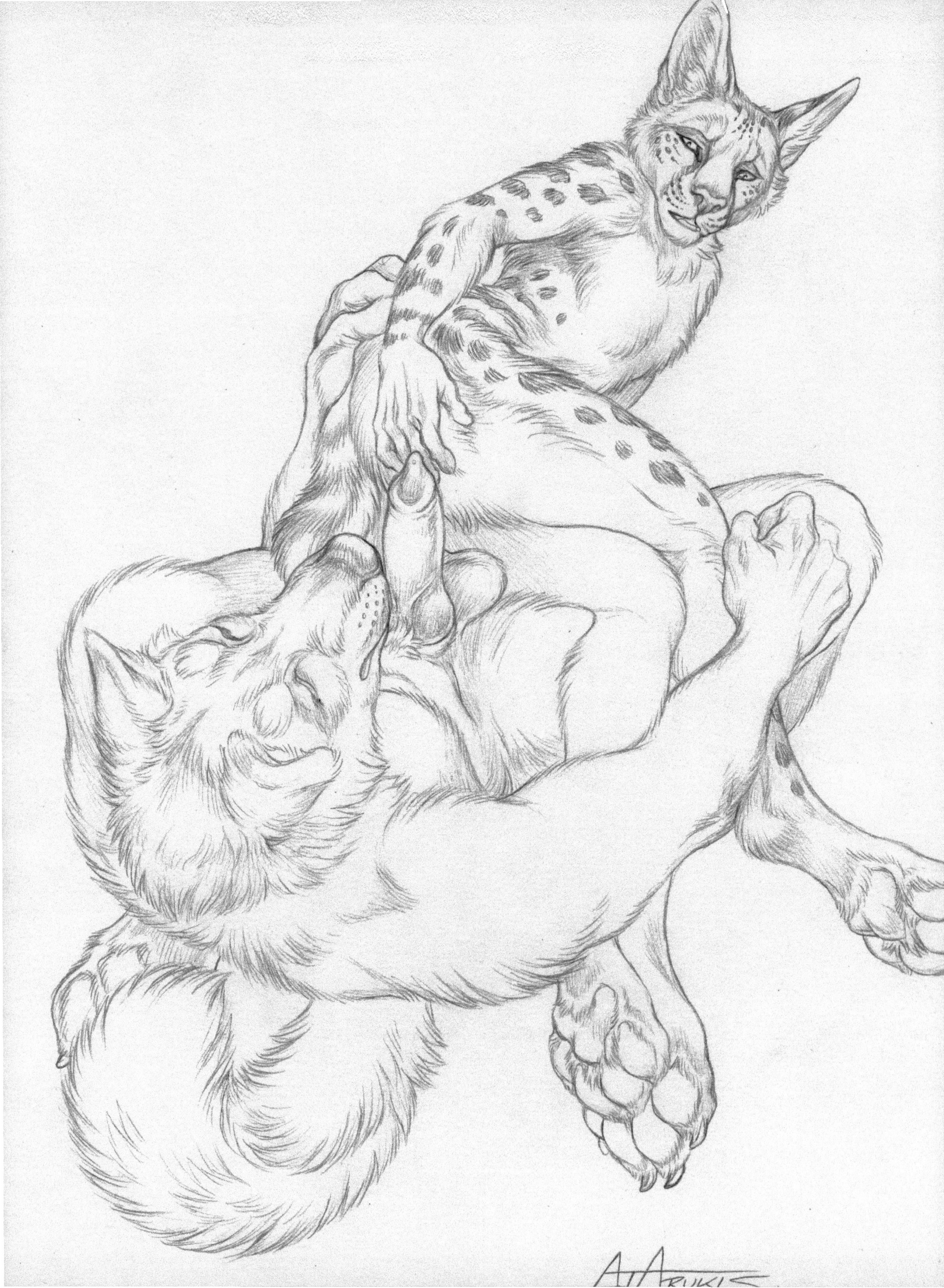

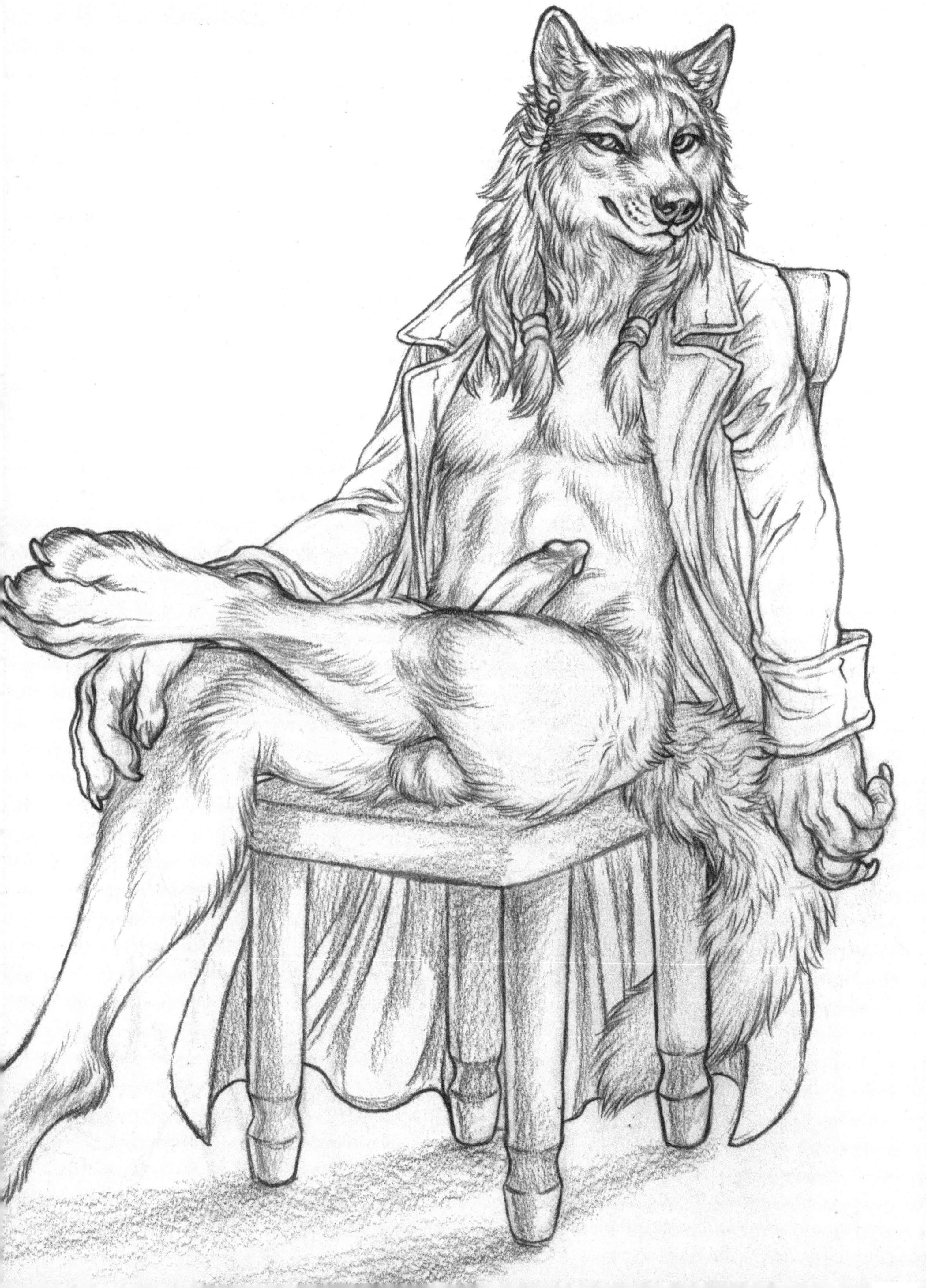

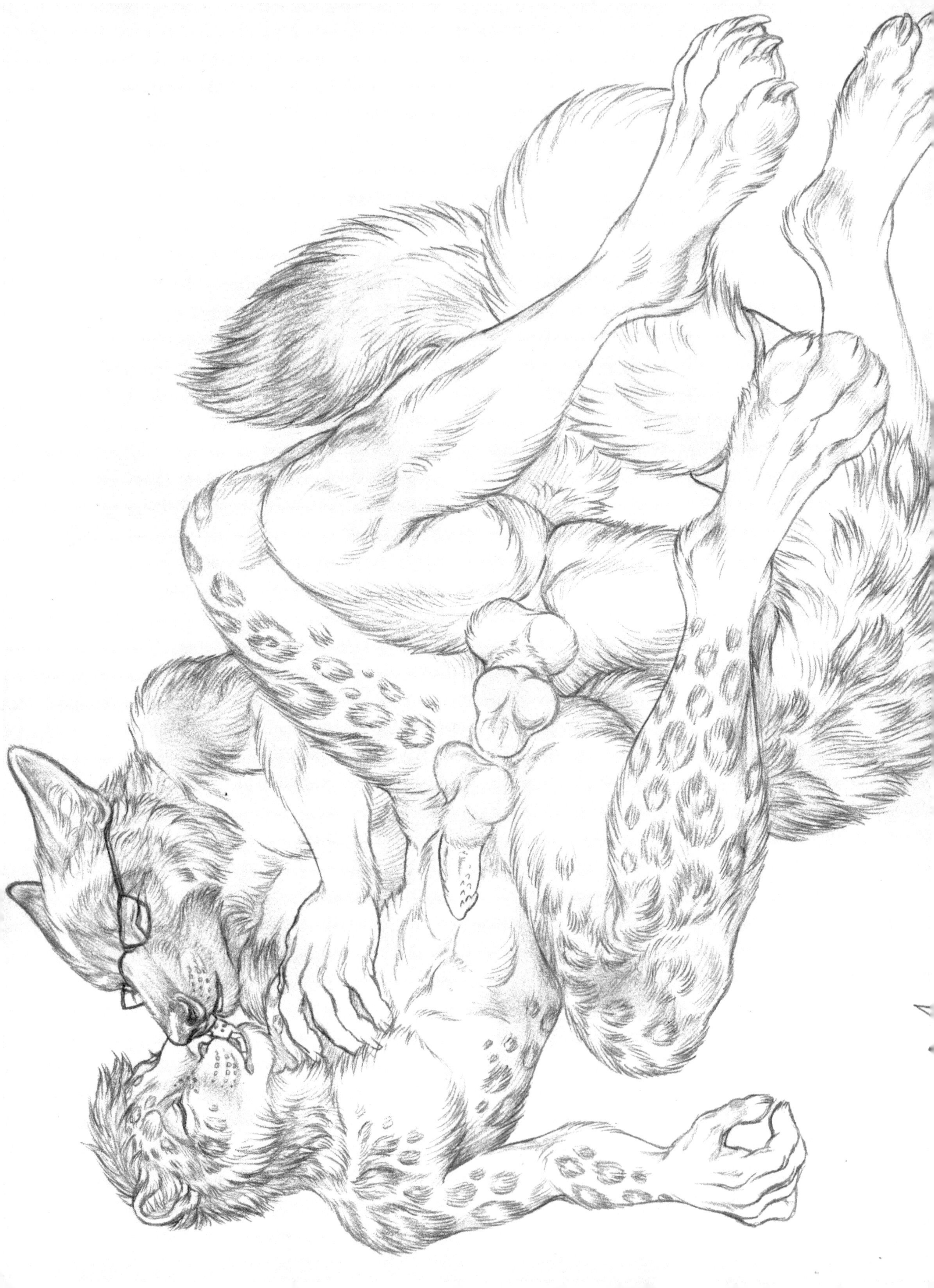

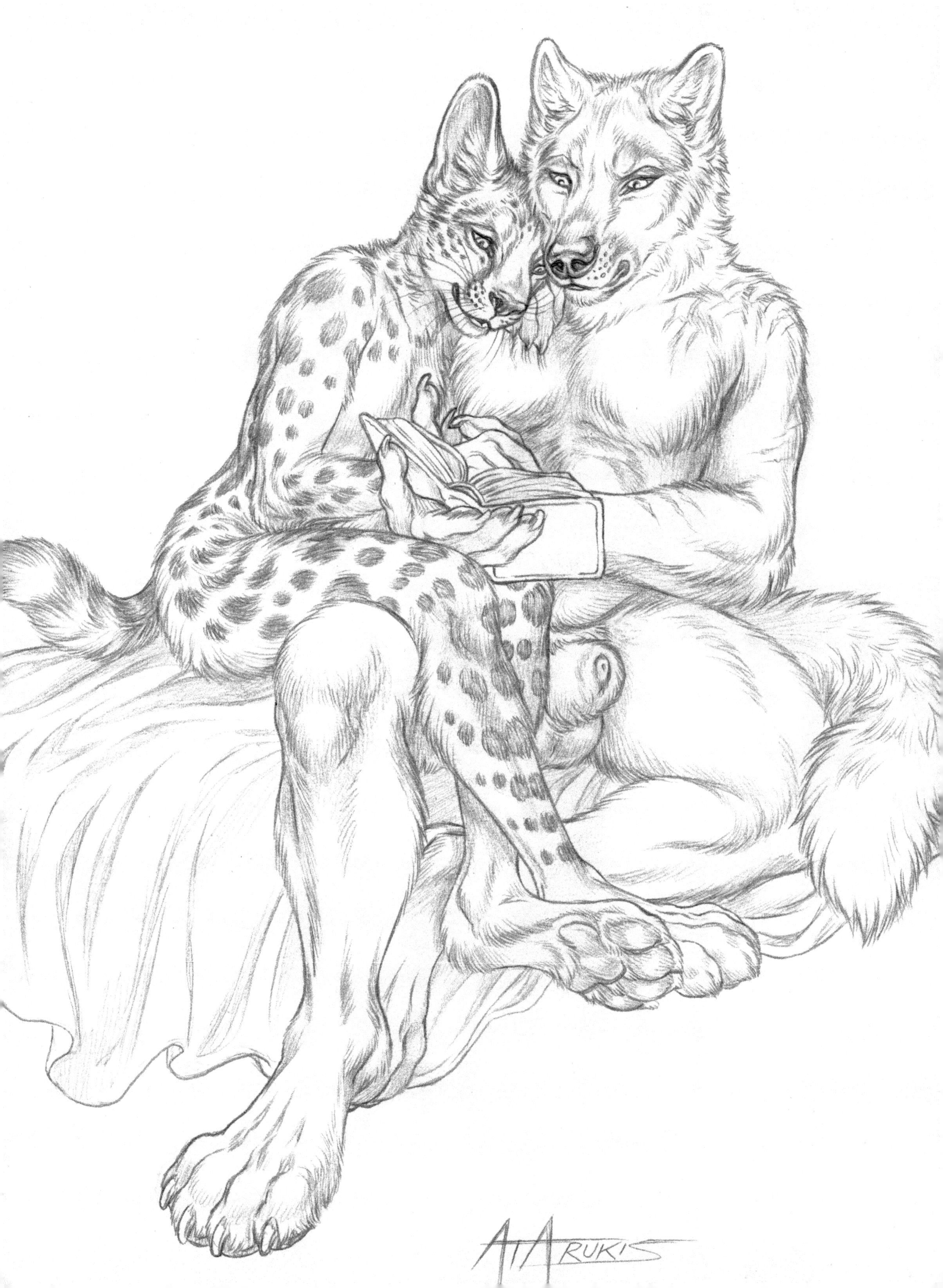

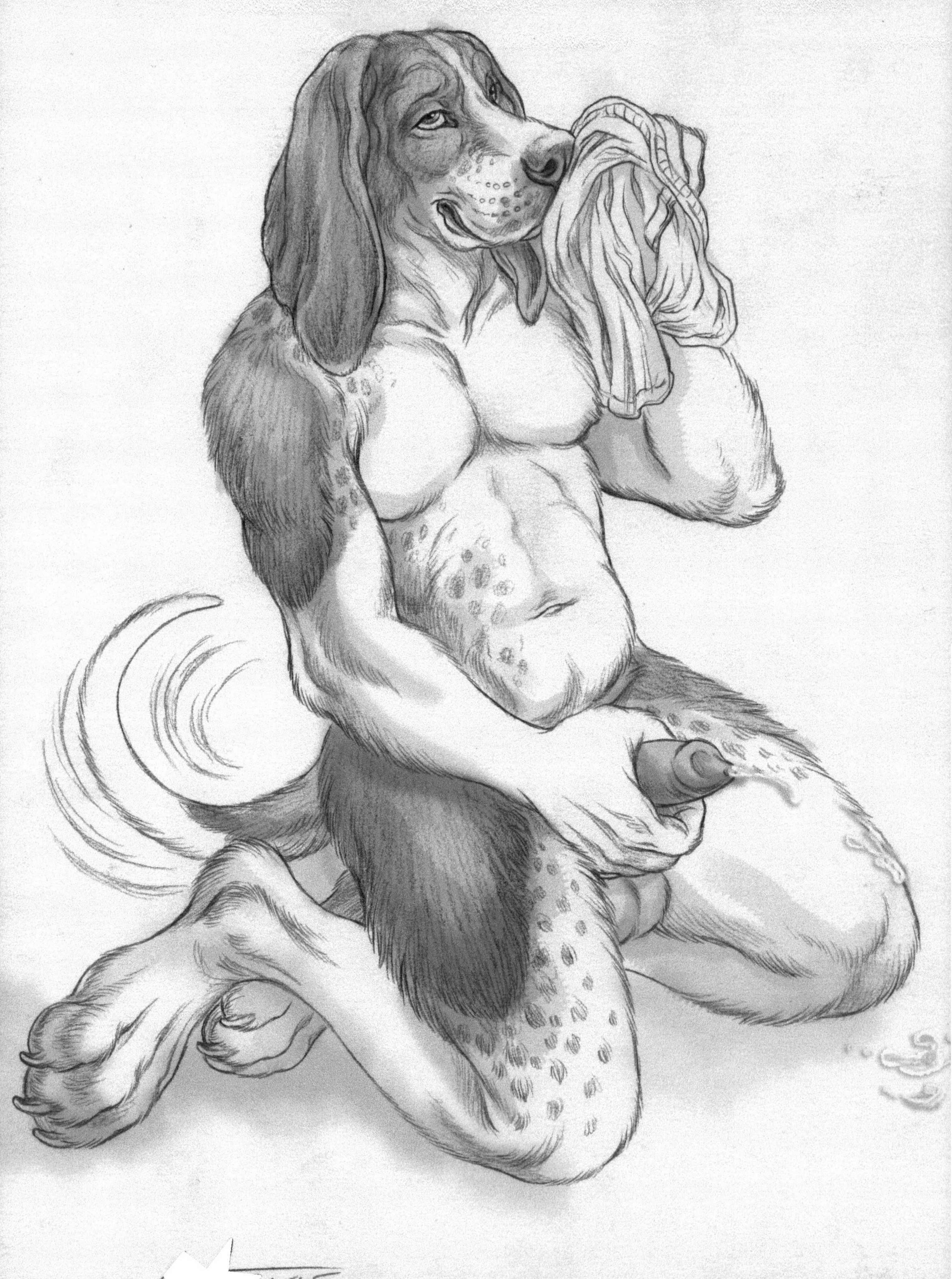

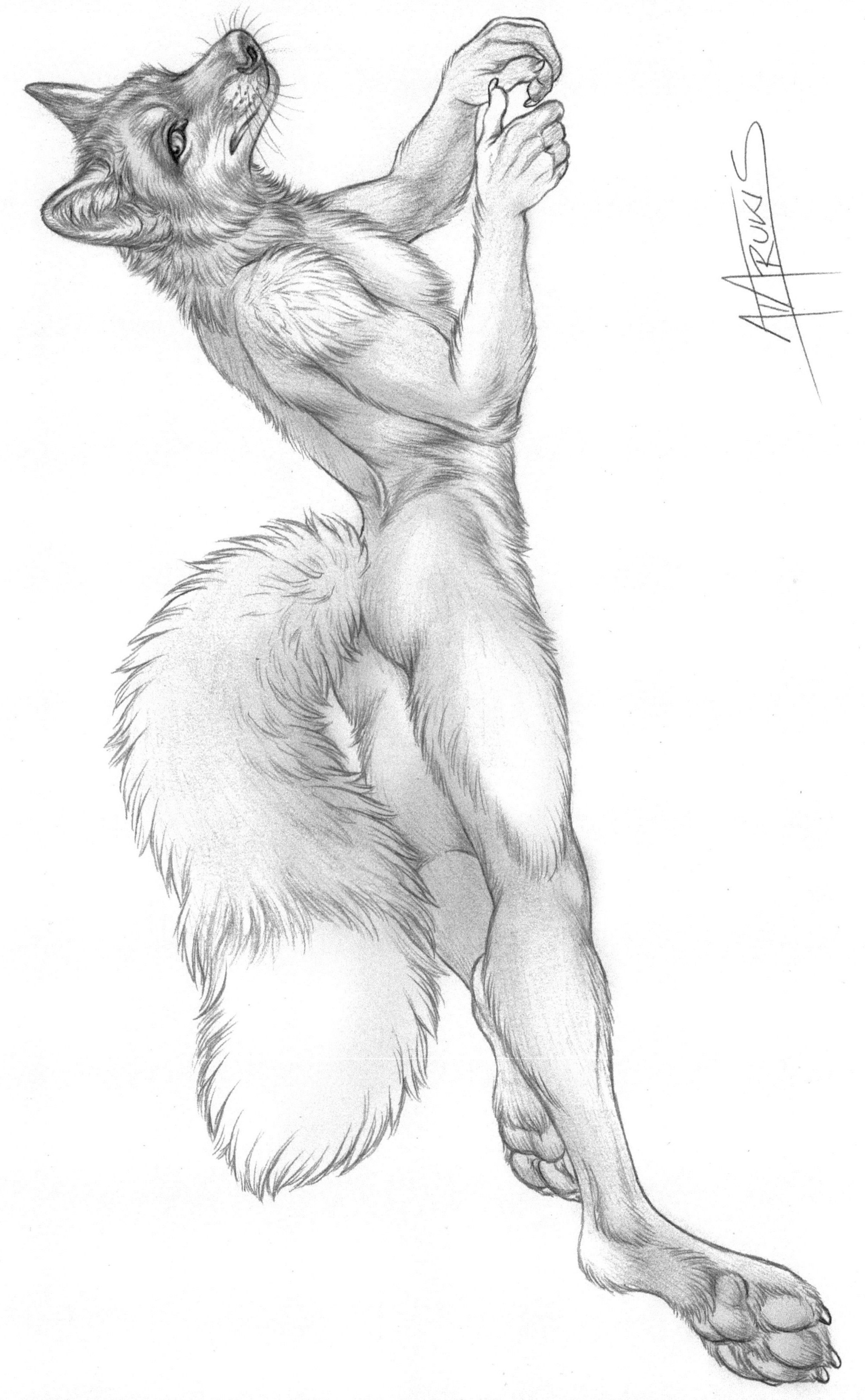

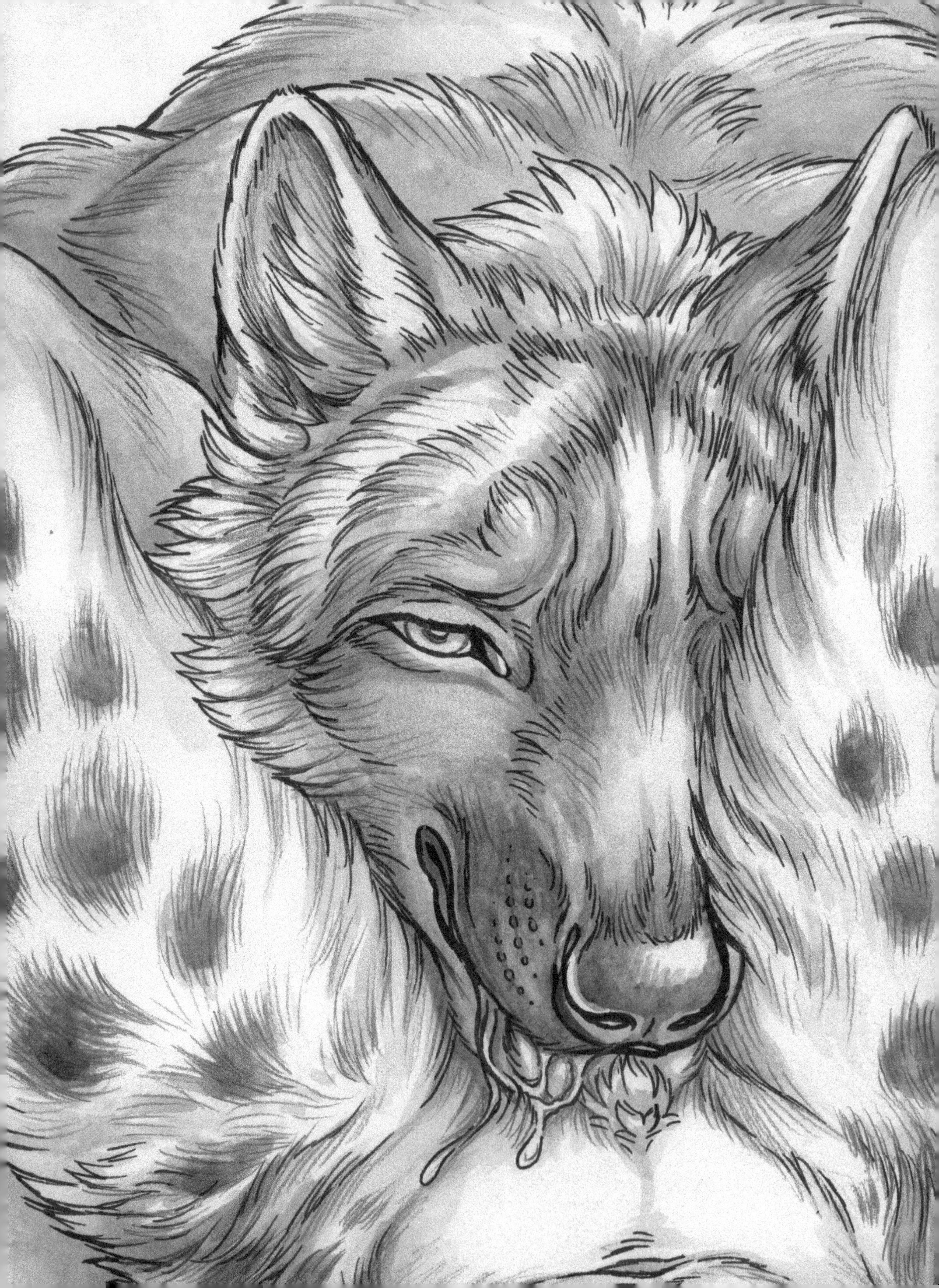

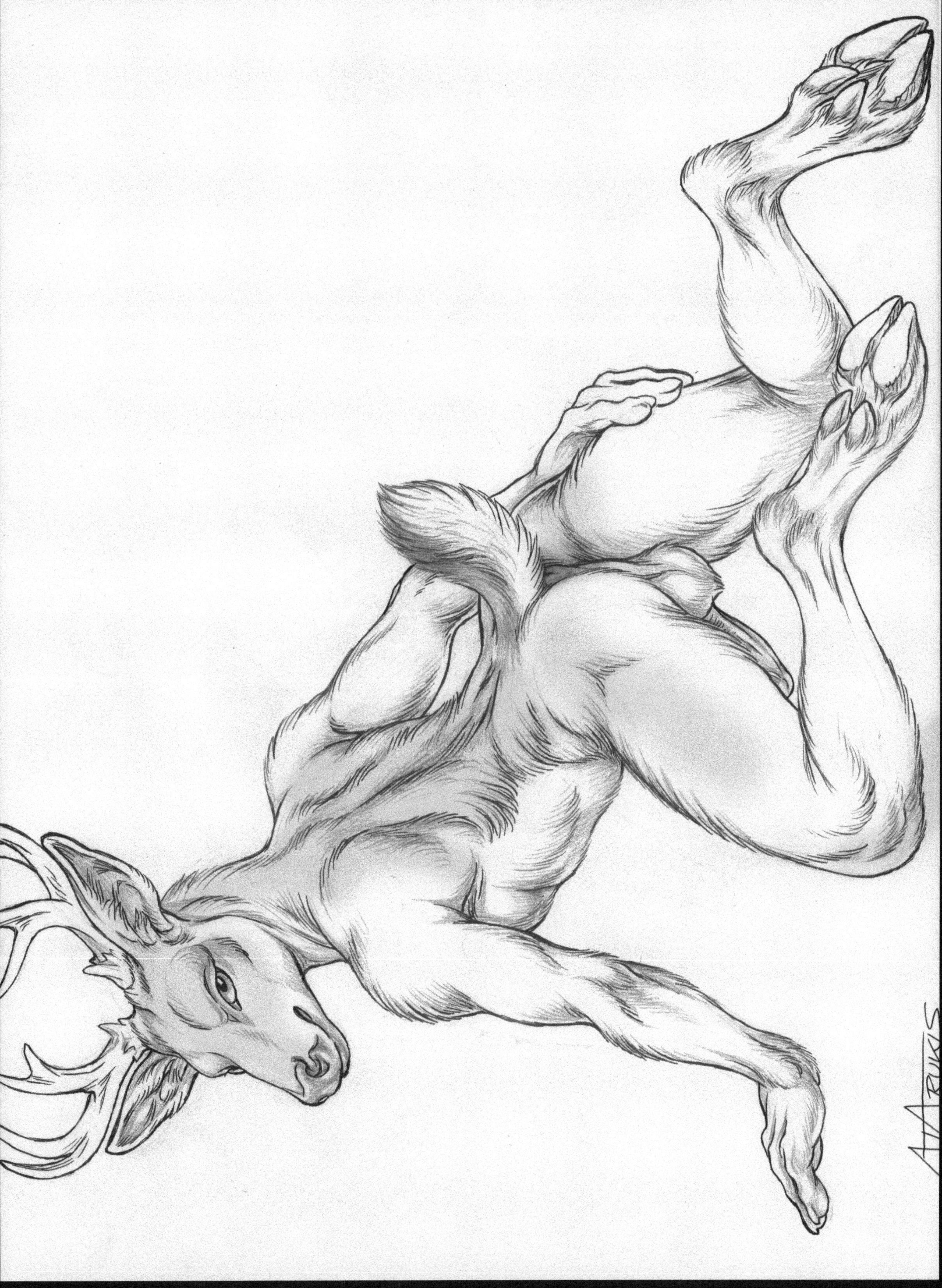

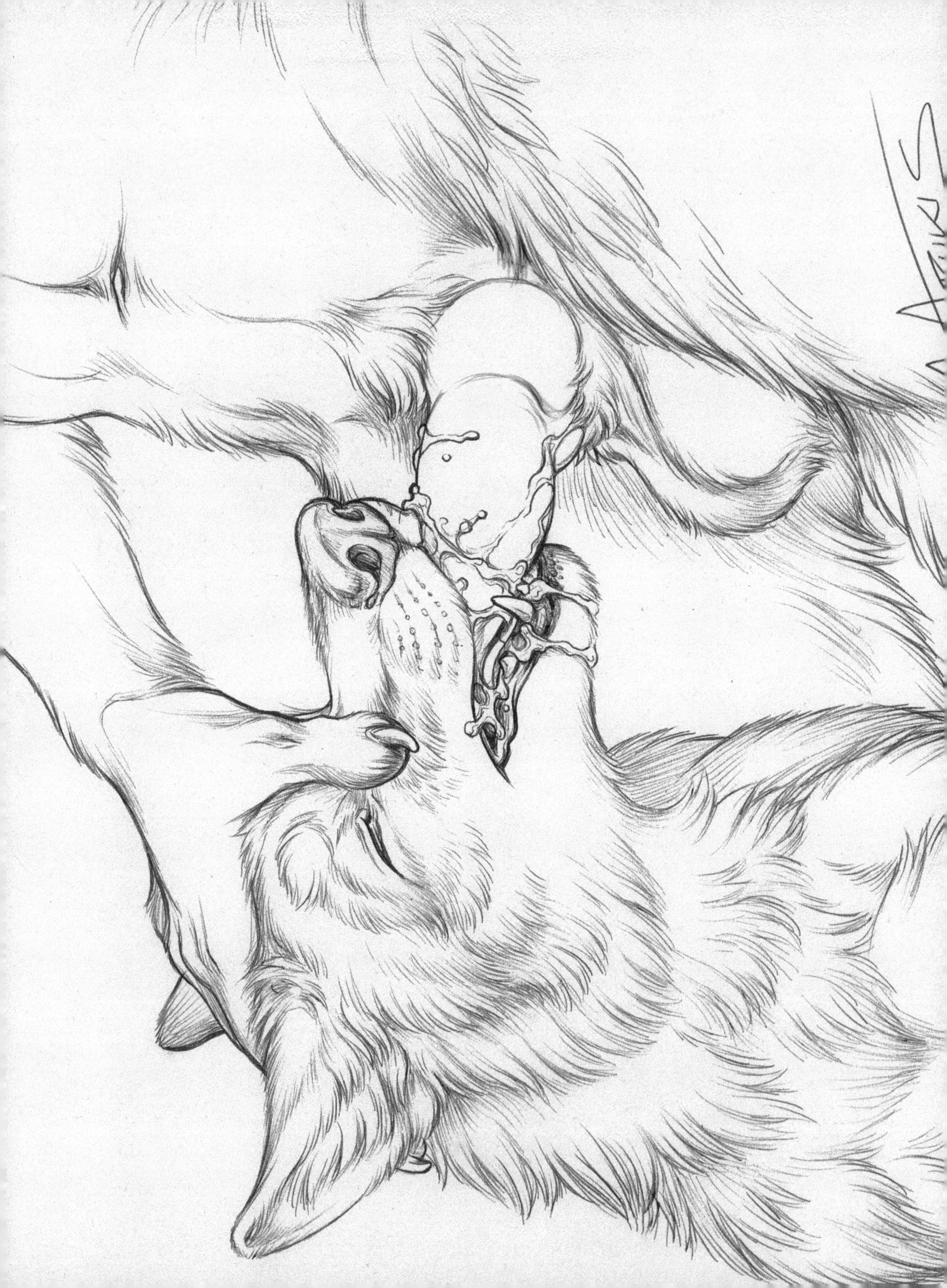

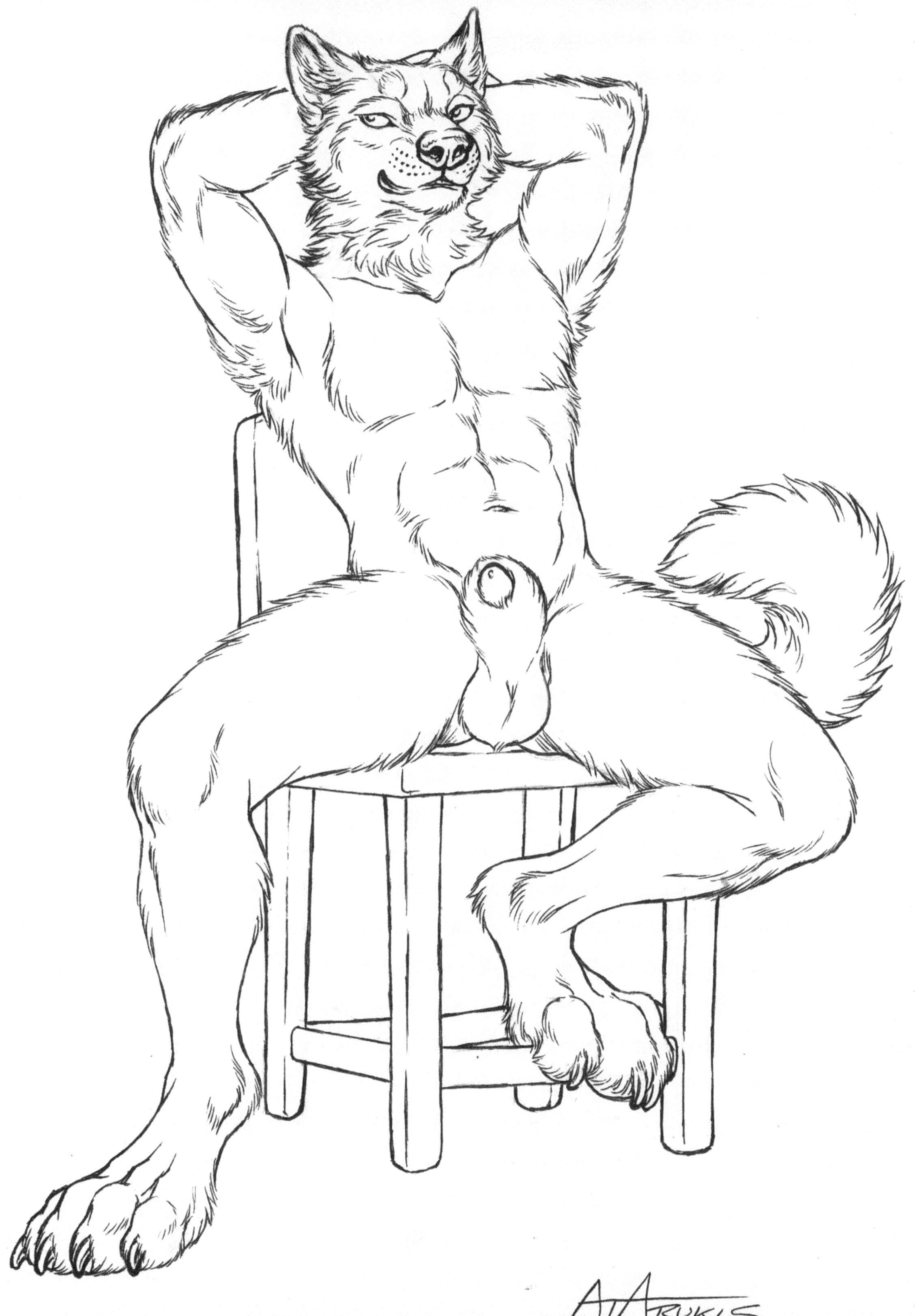

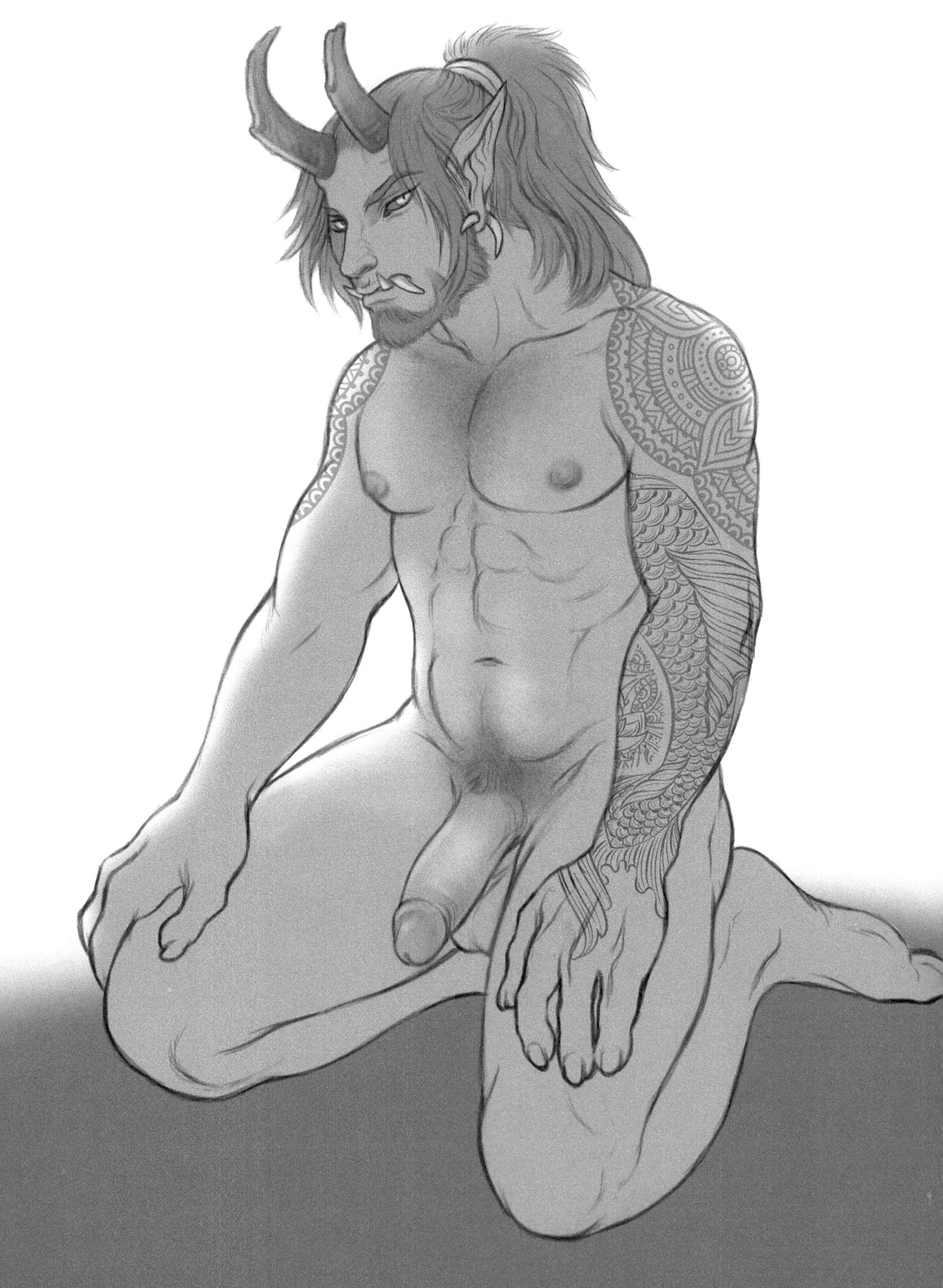

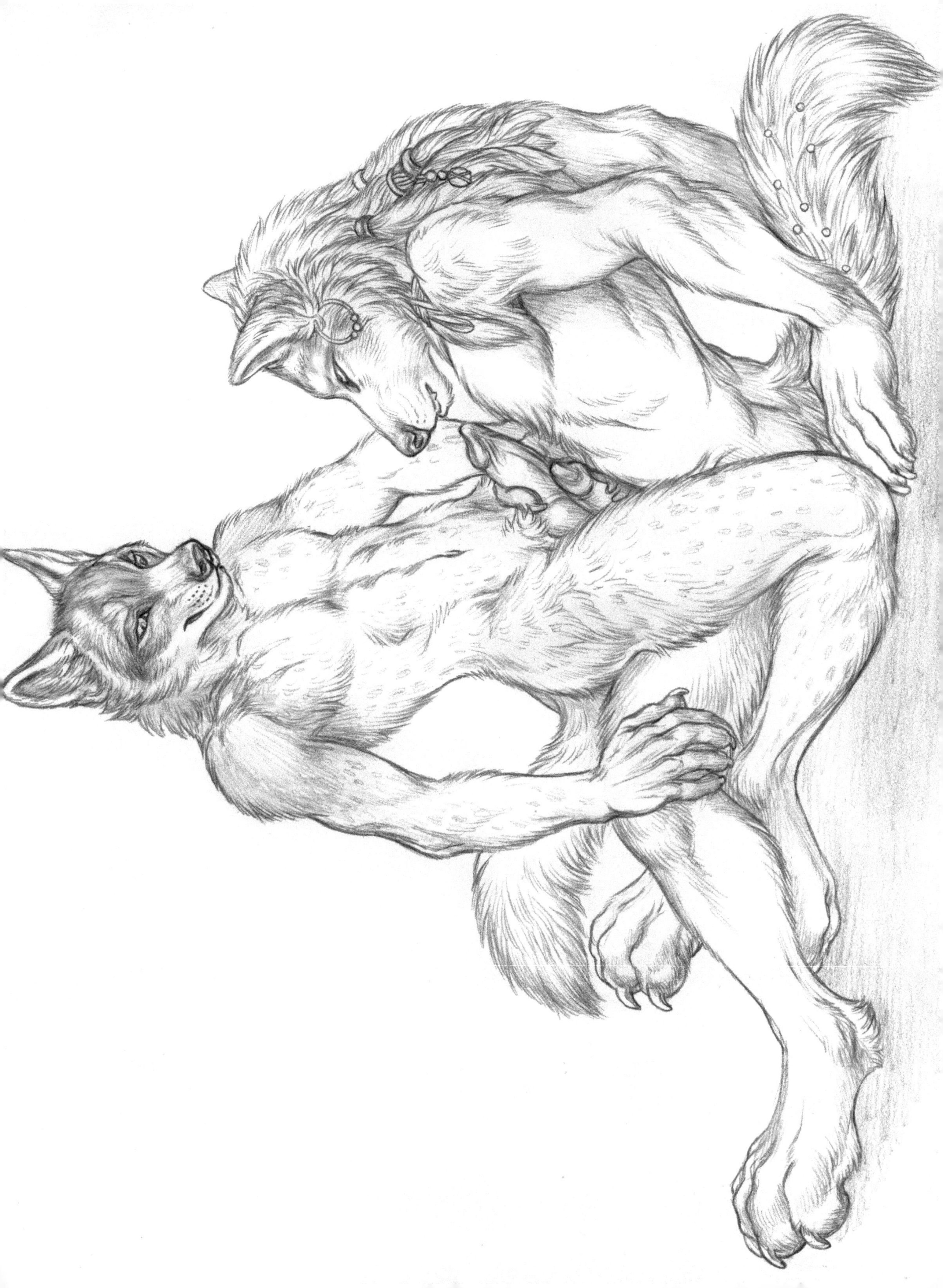

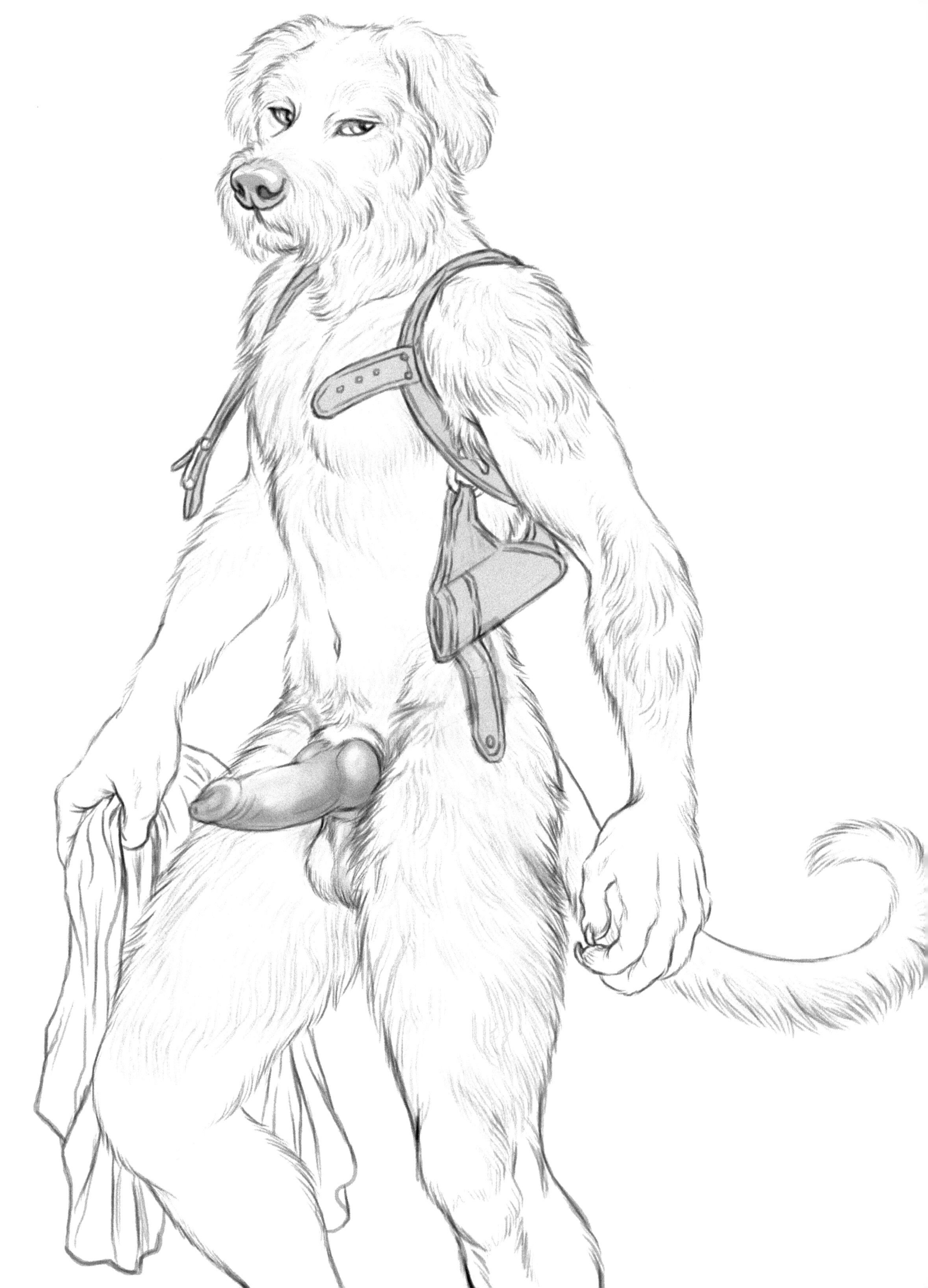

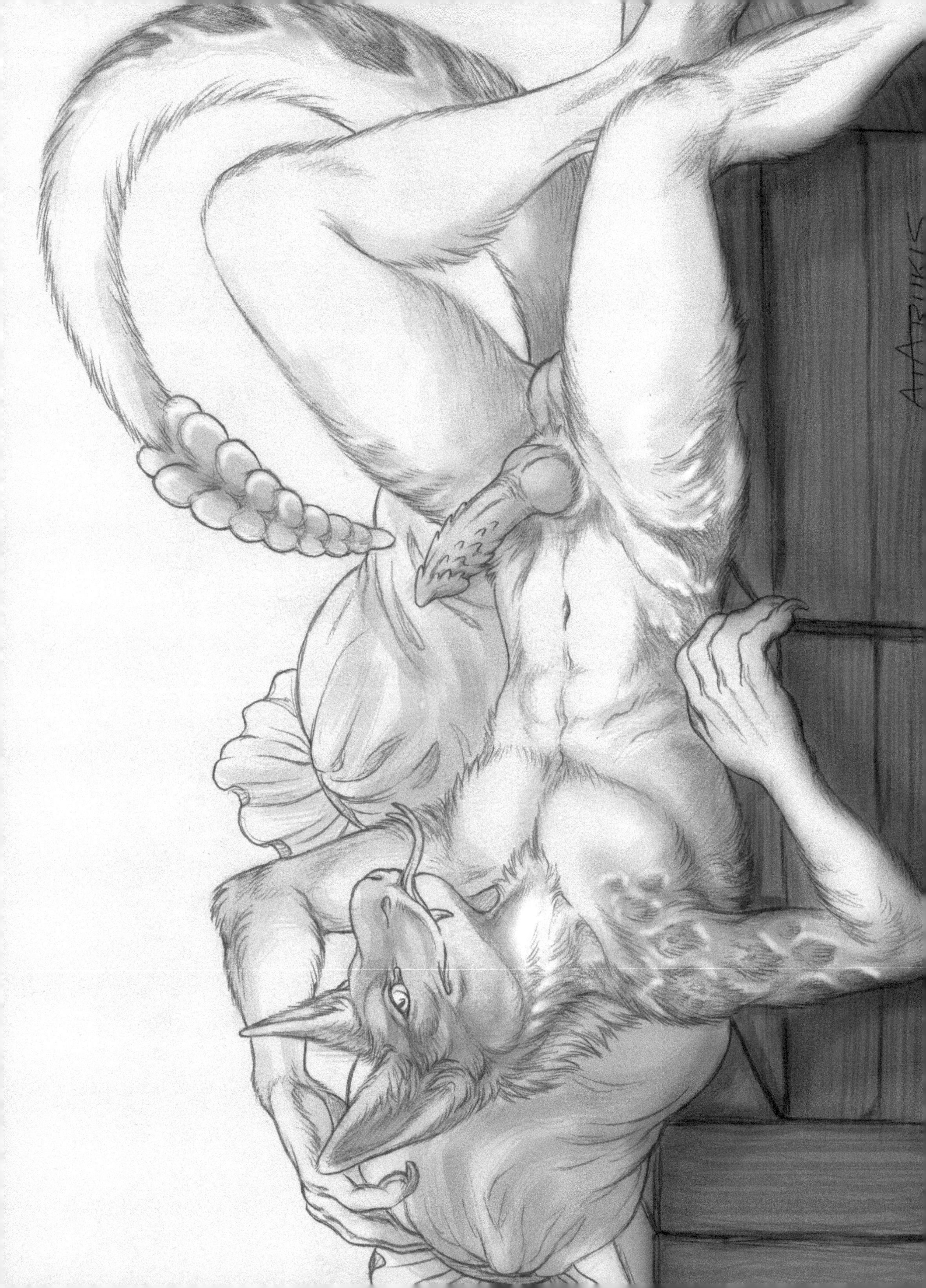

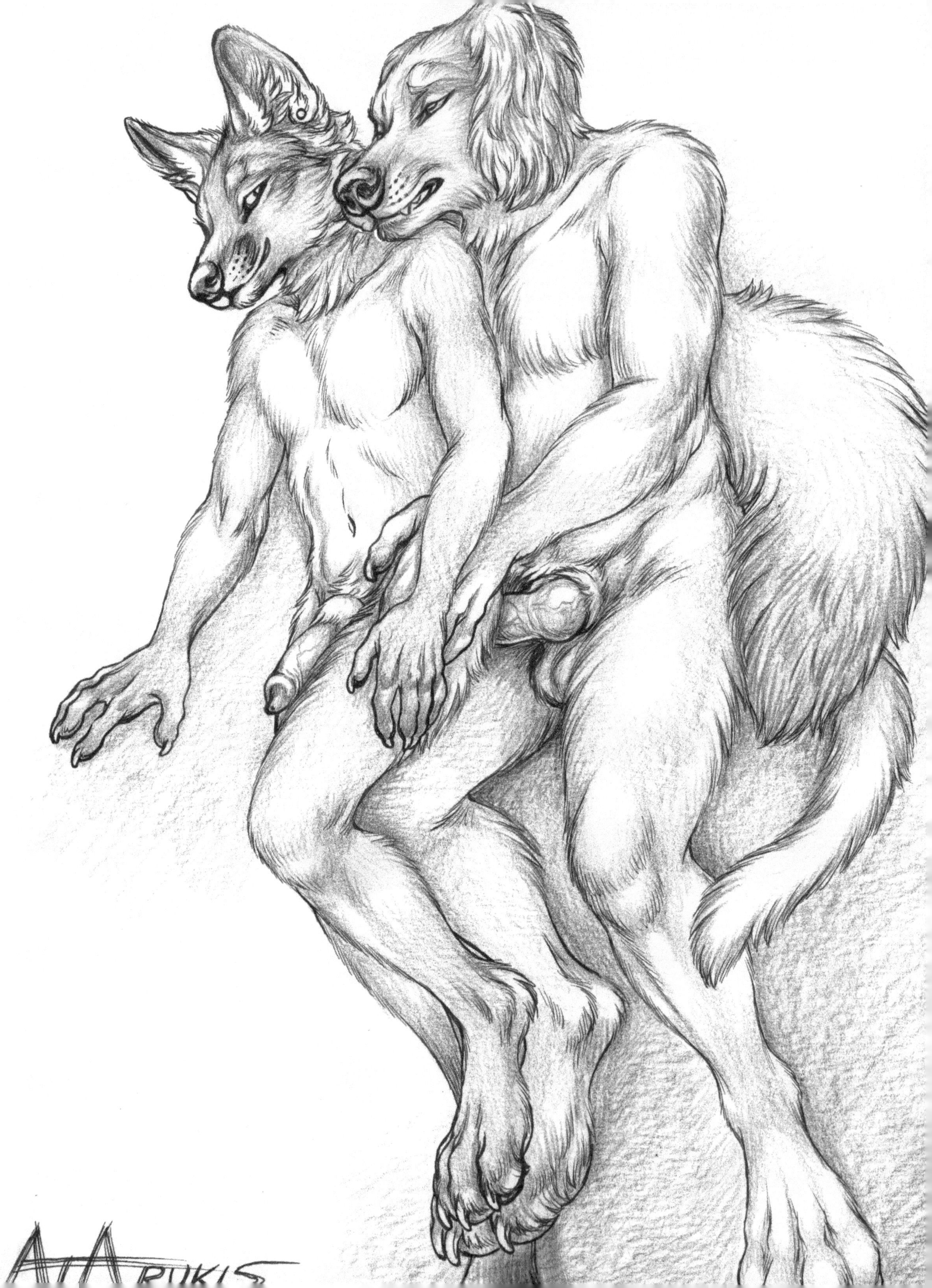

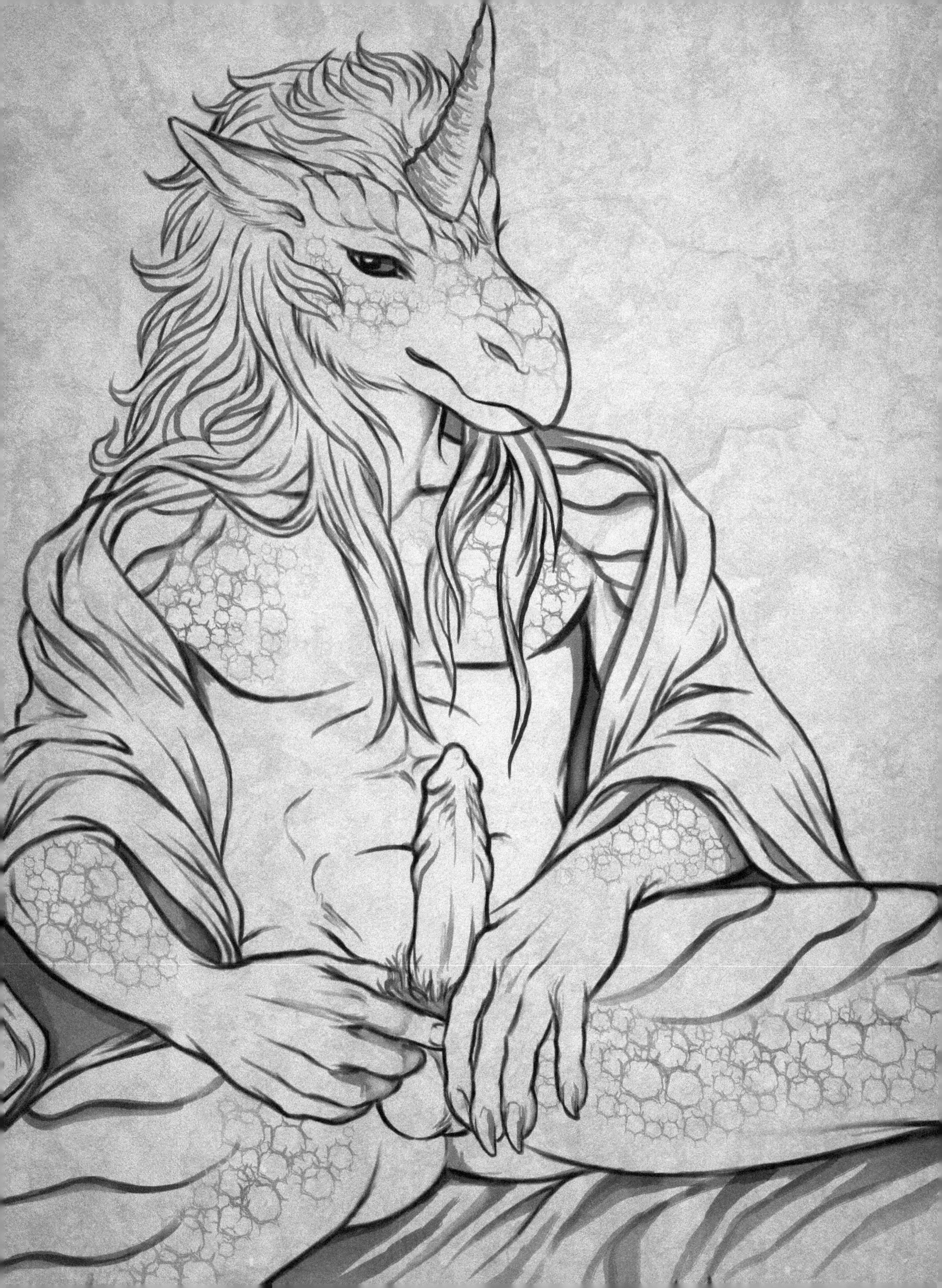

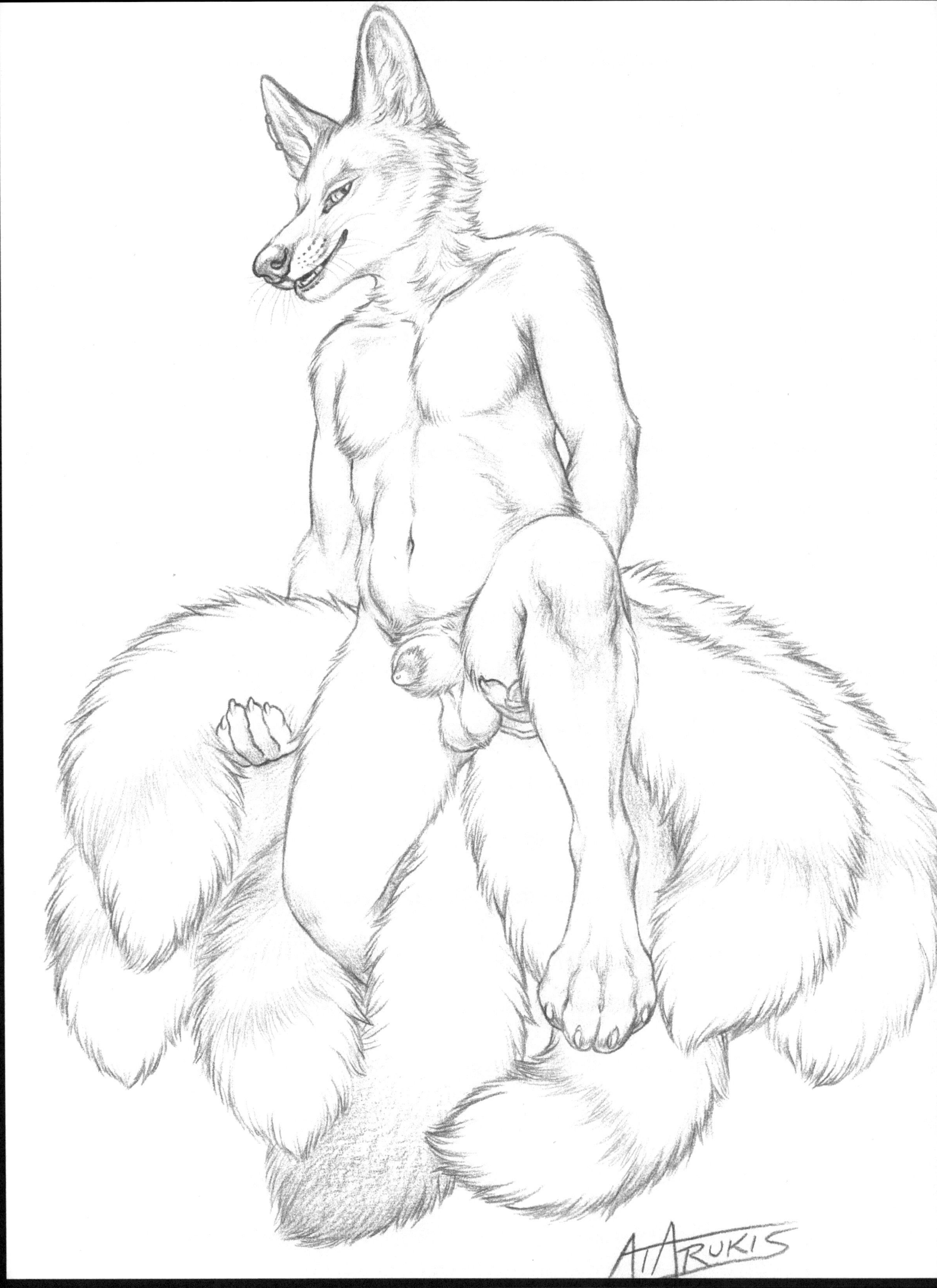

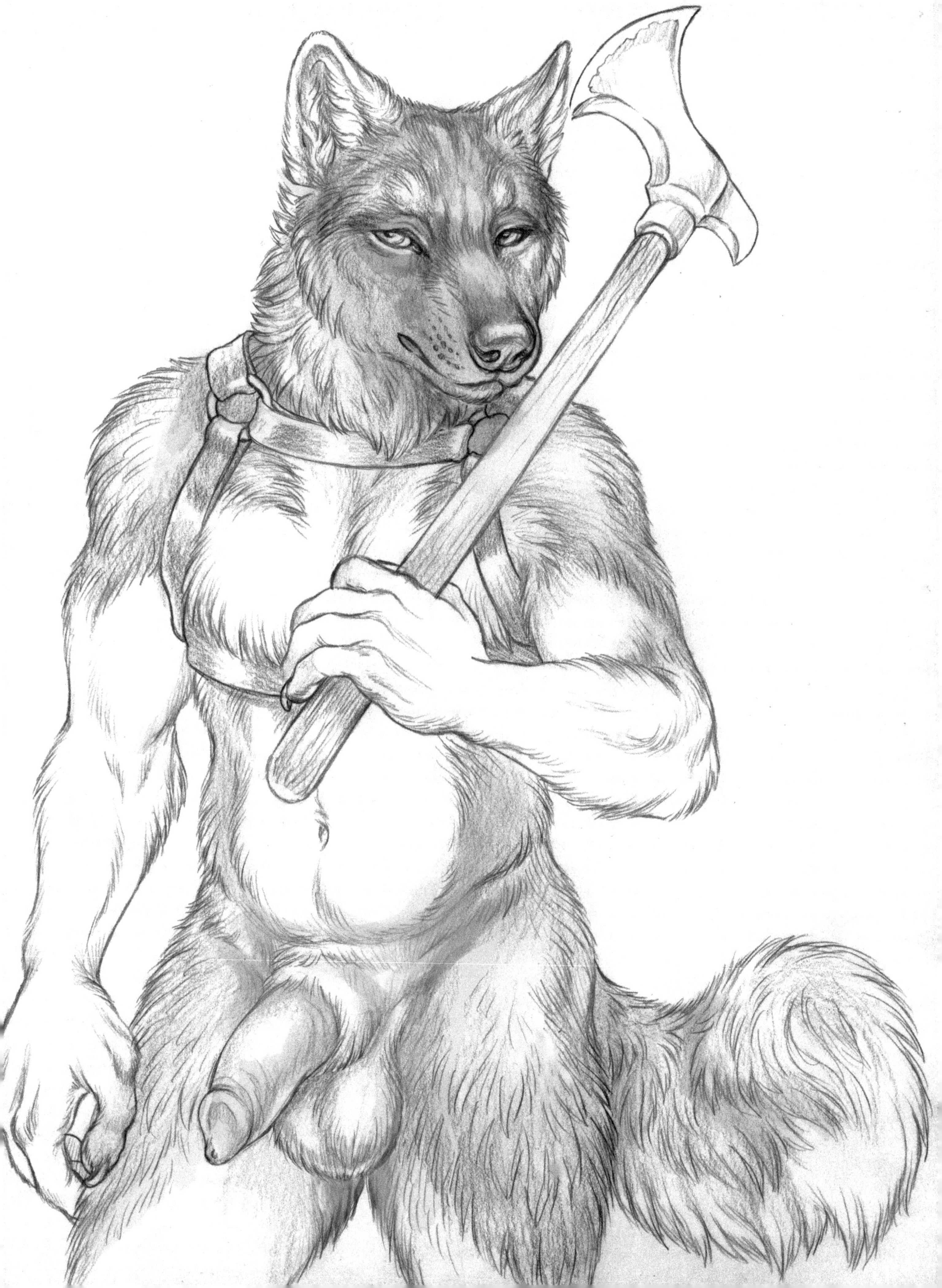

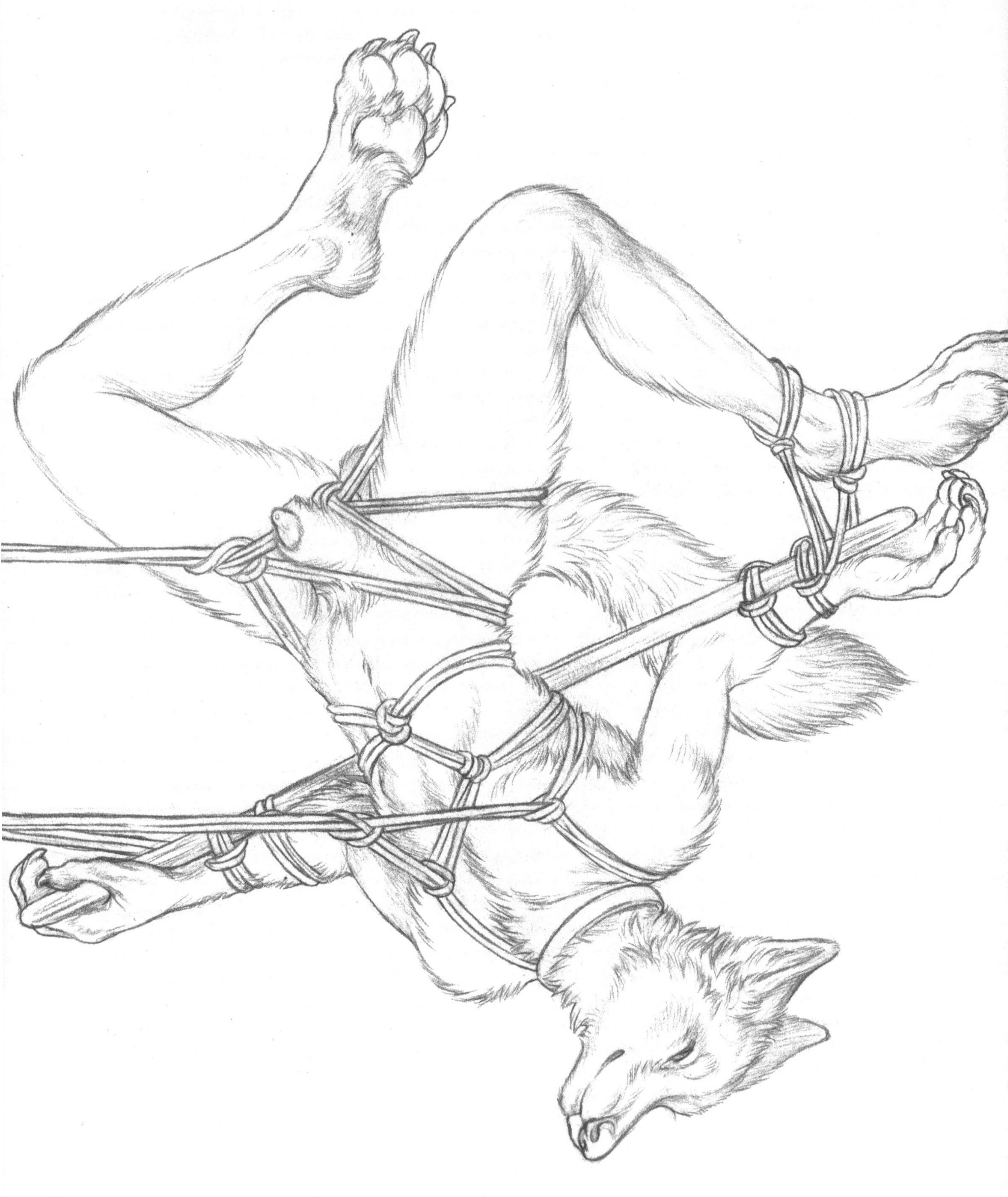

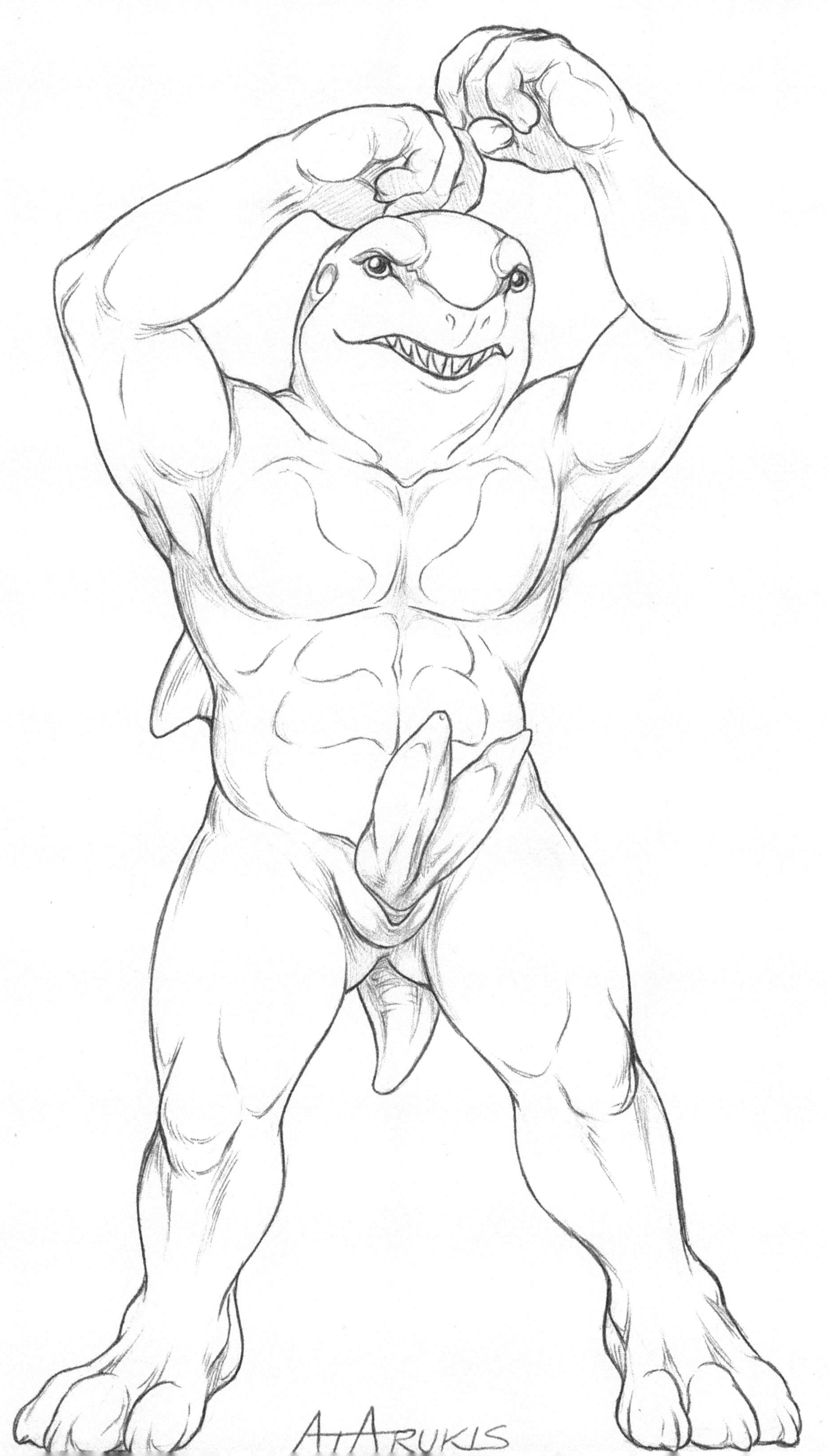

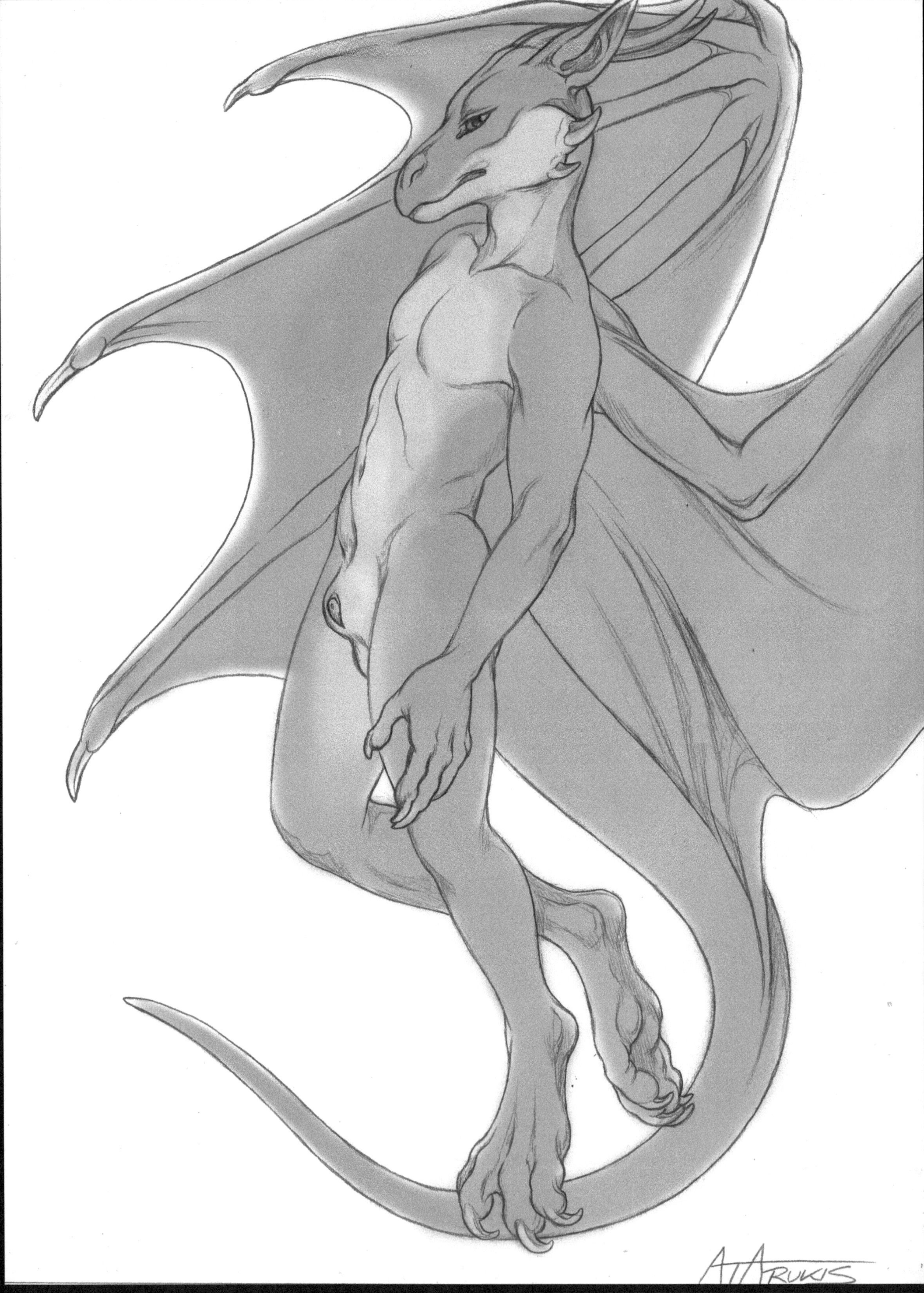
ATArukis

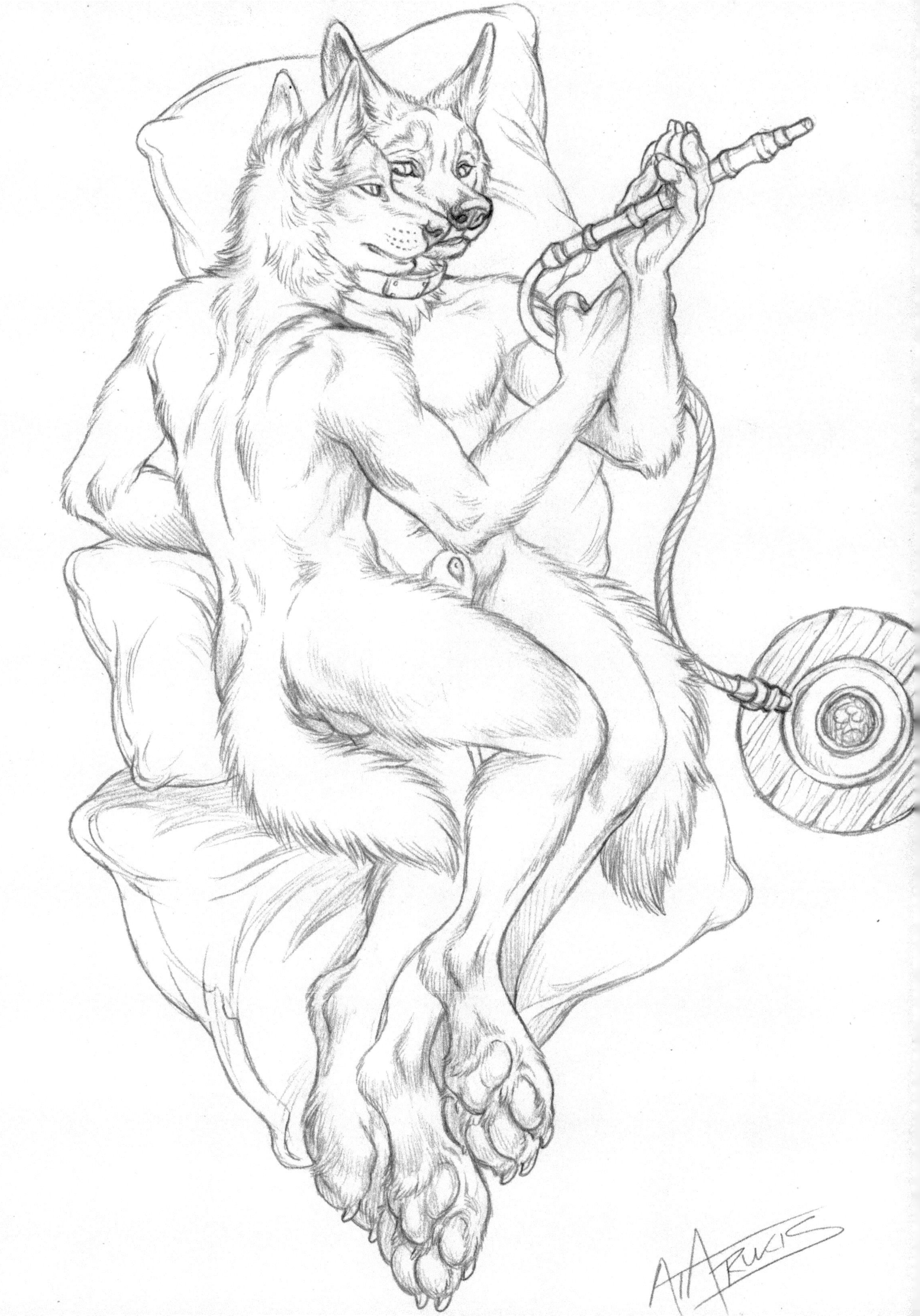

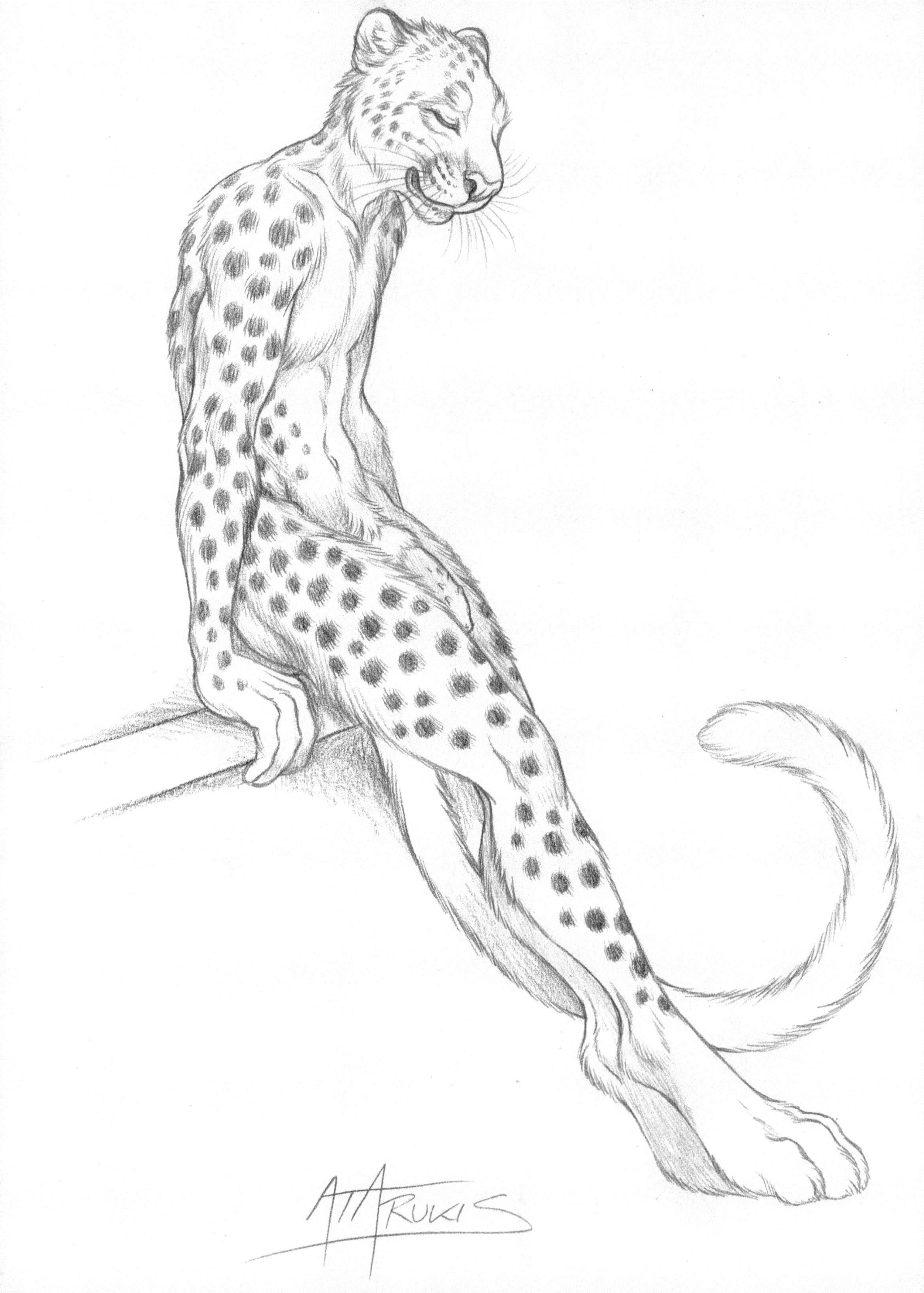

ATArukis

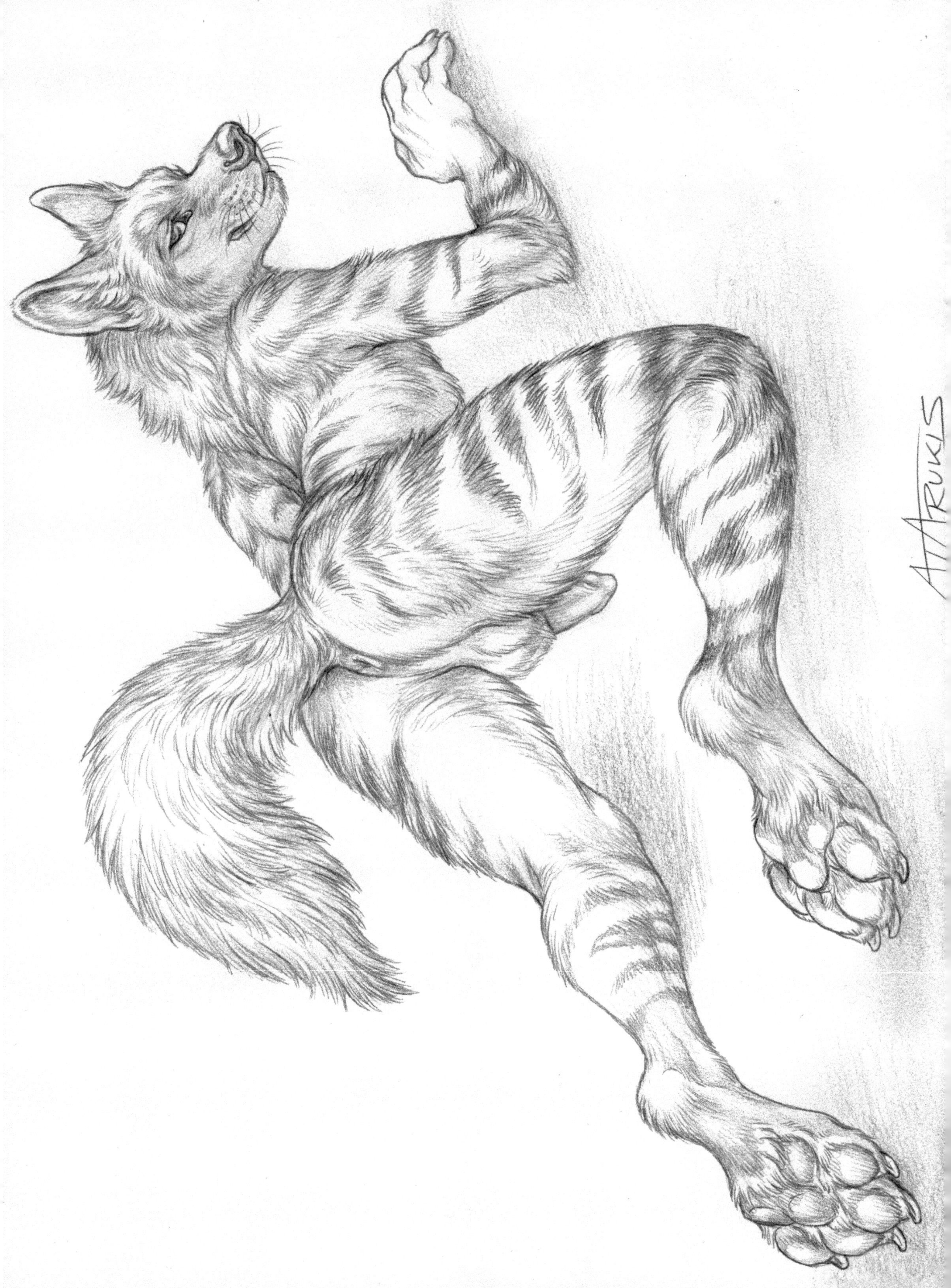

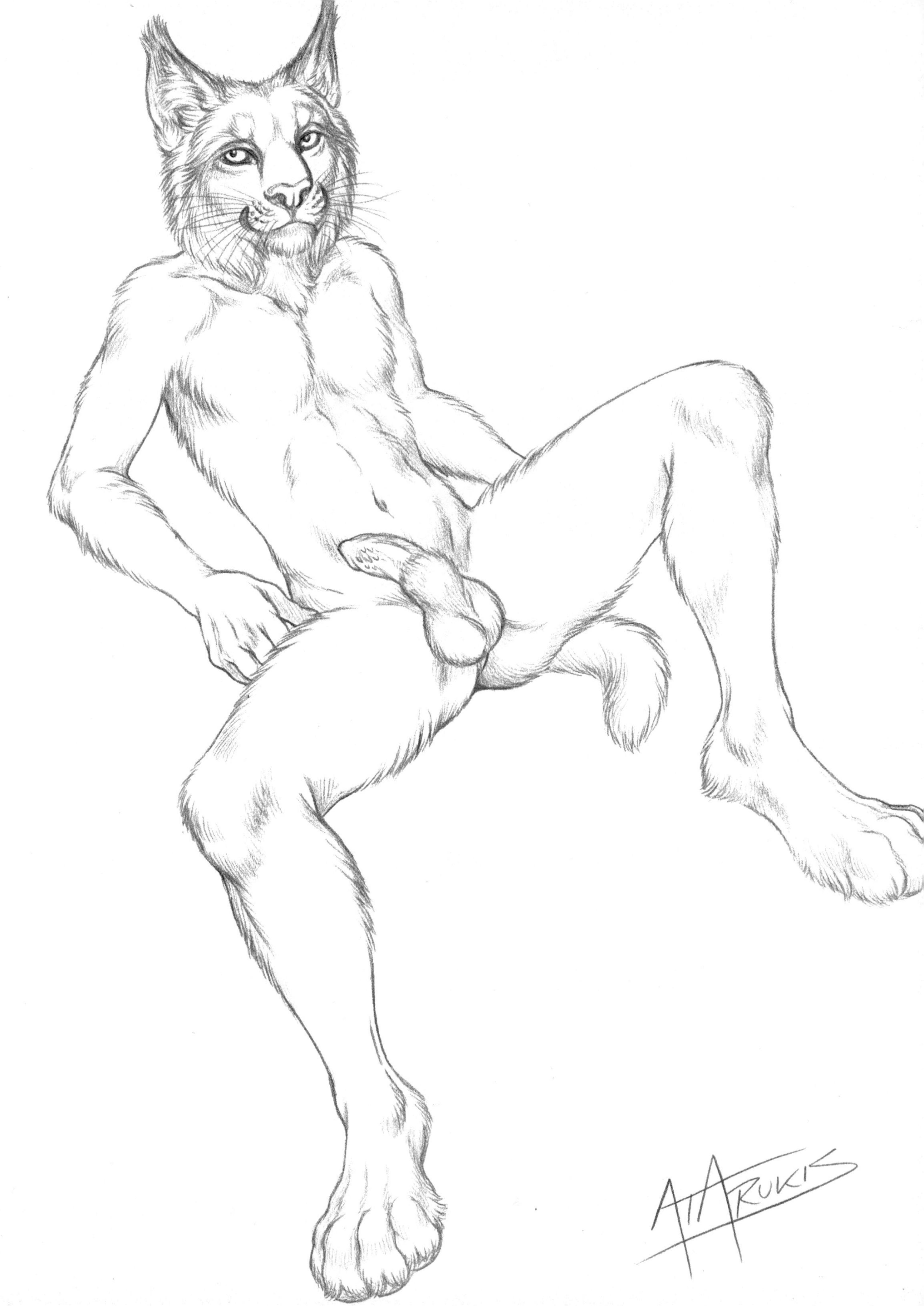

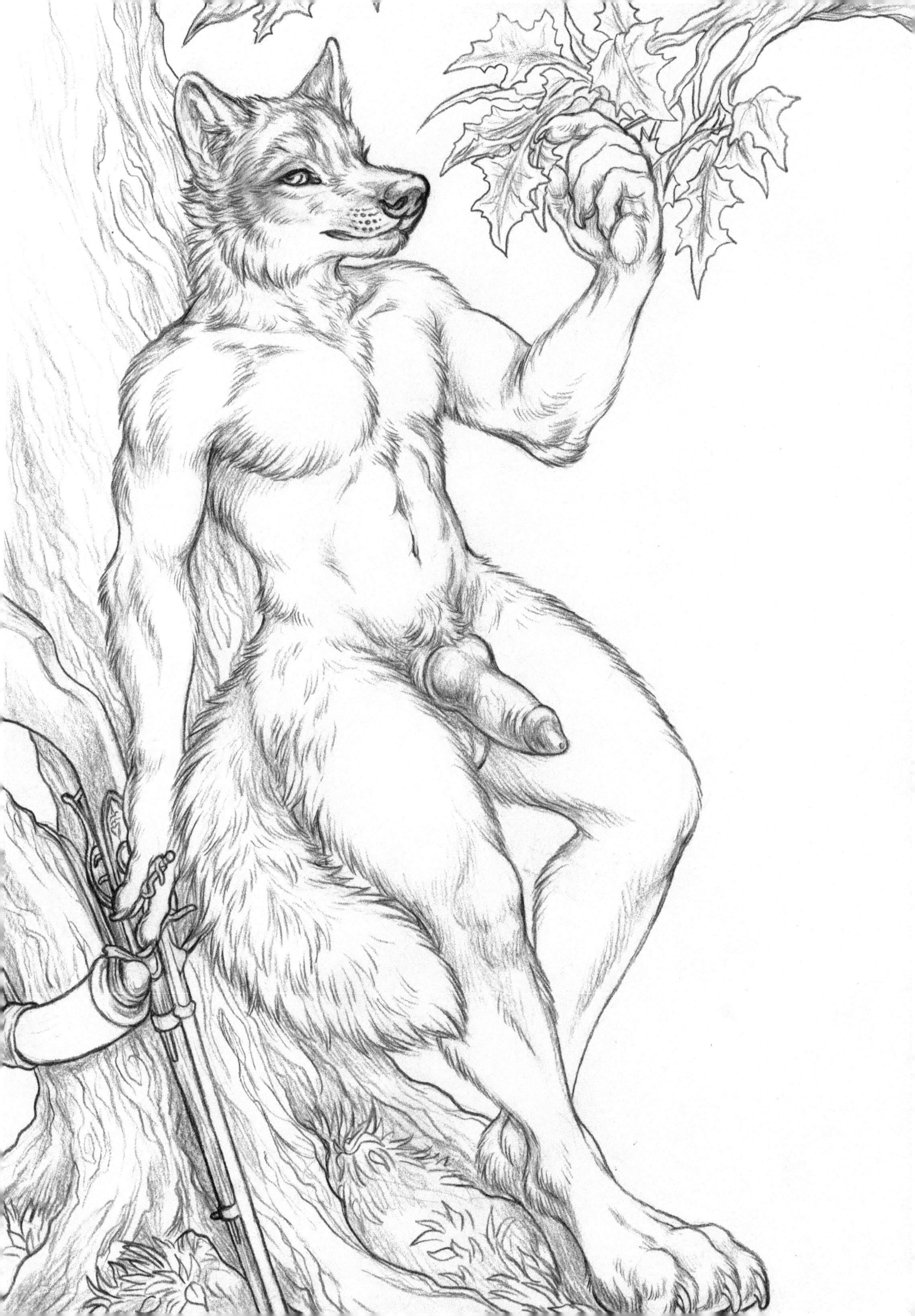

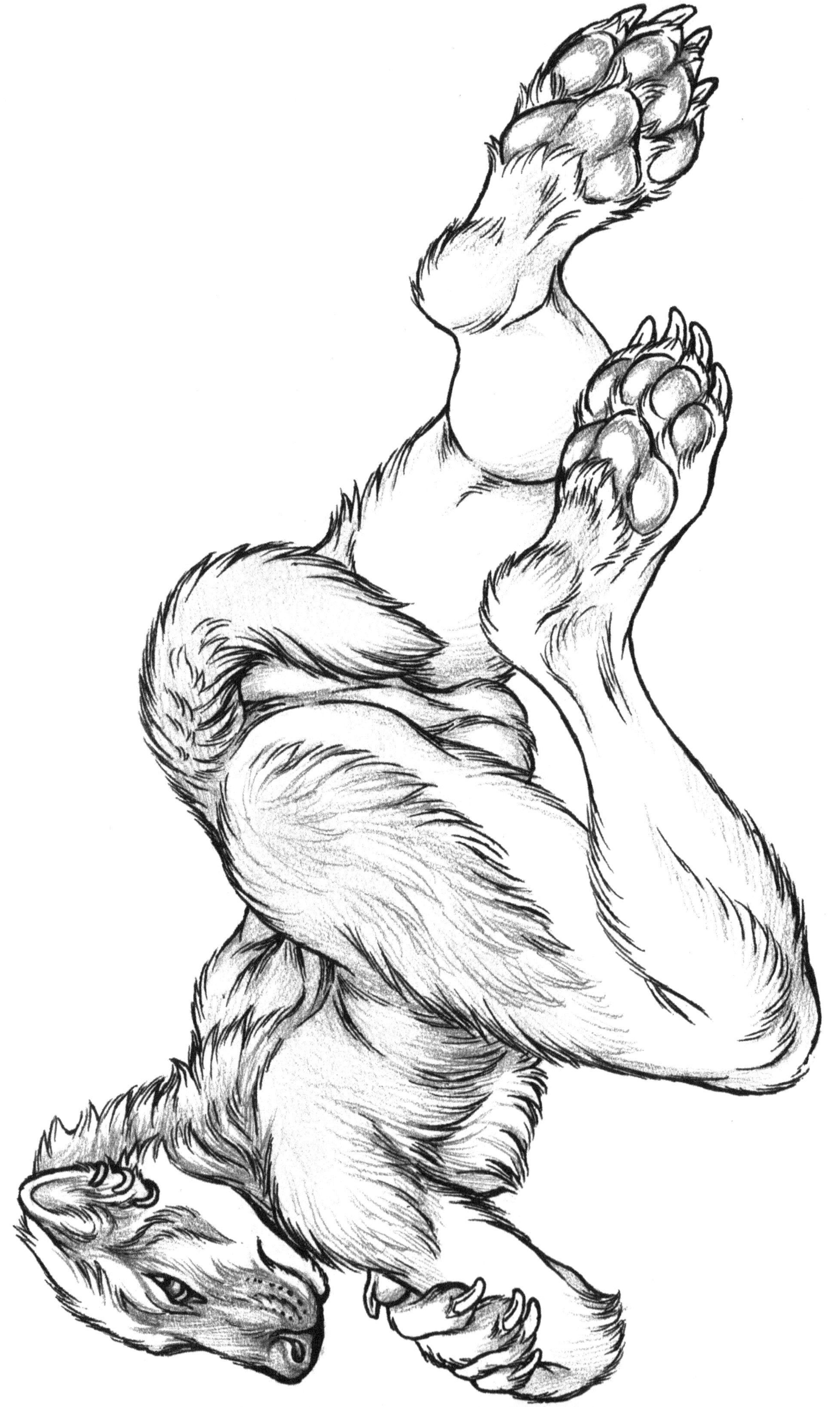

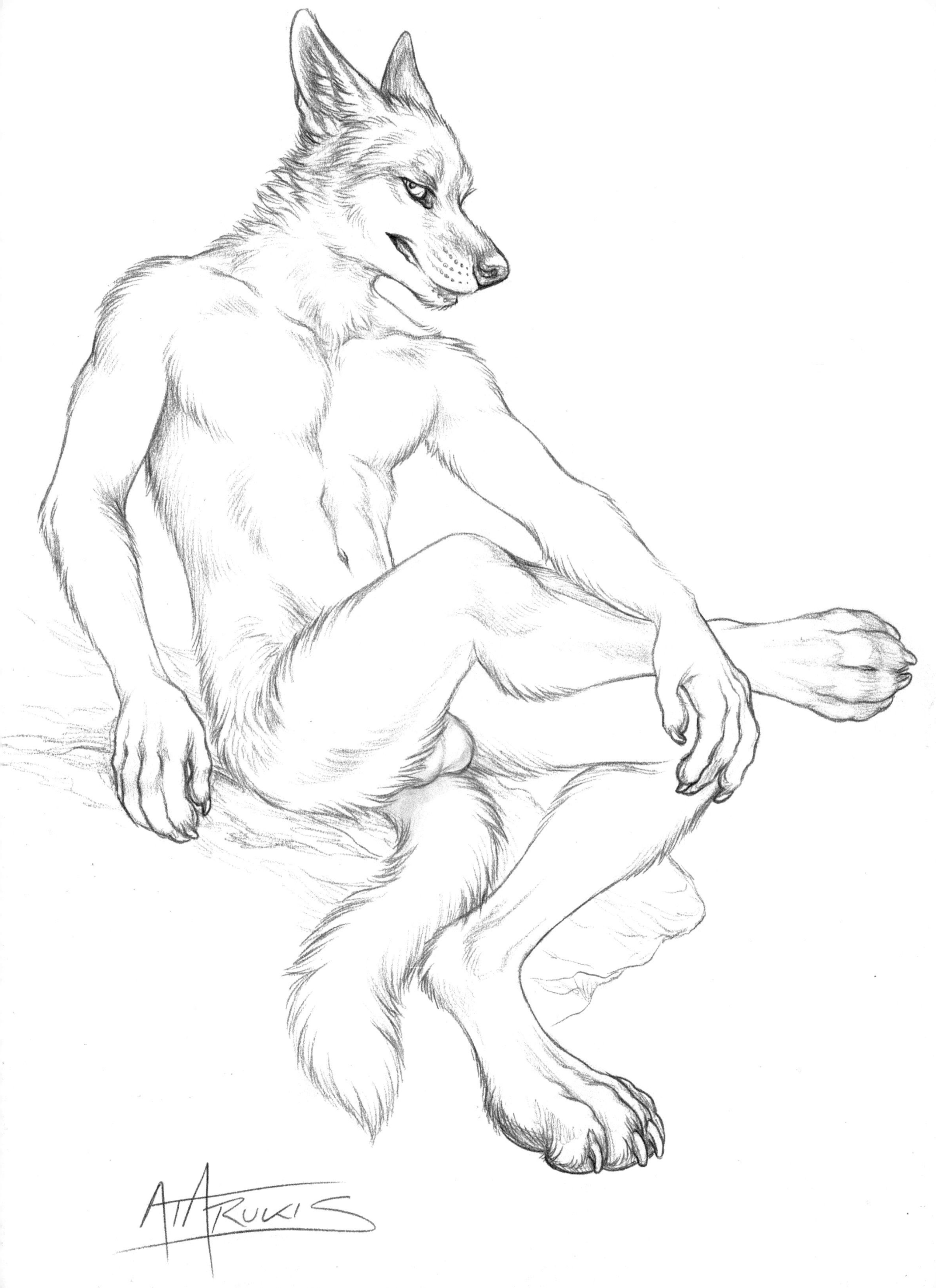

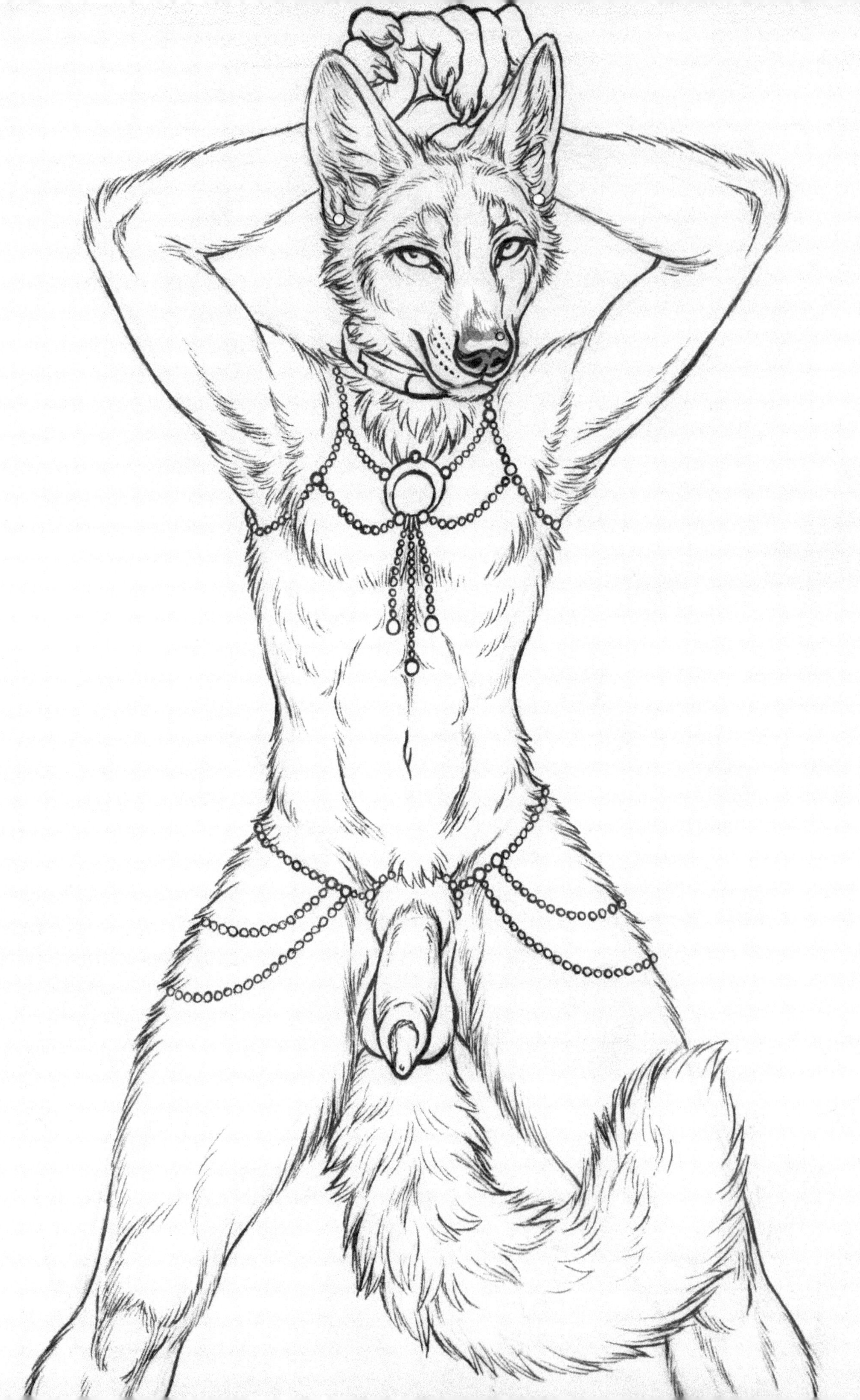

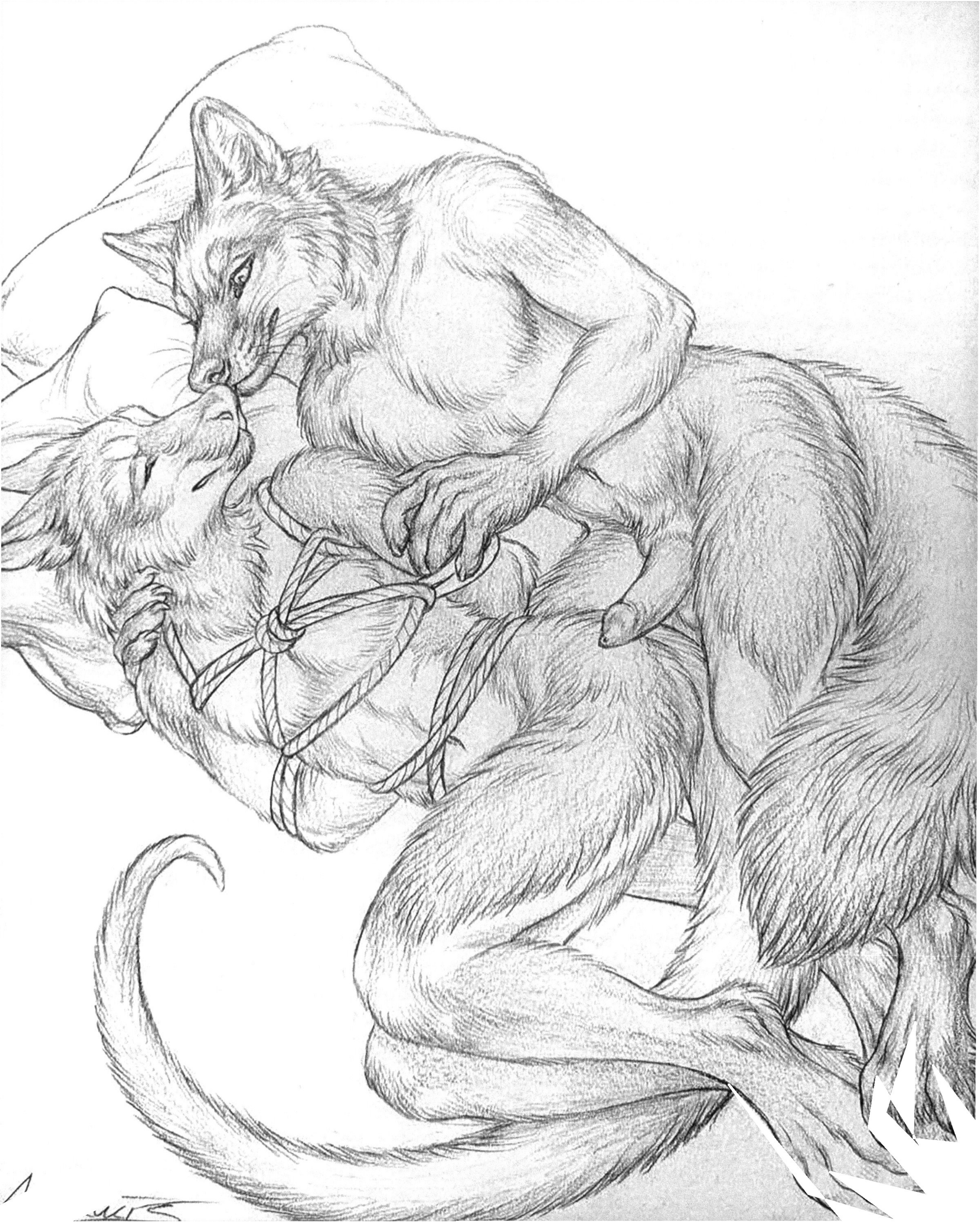

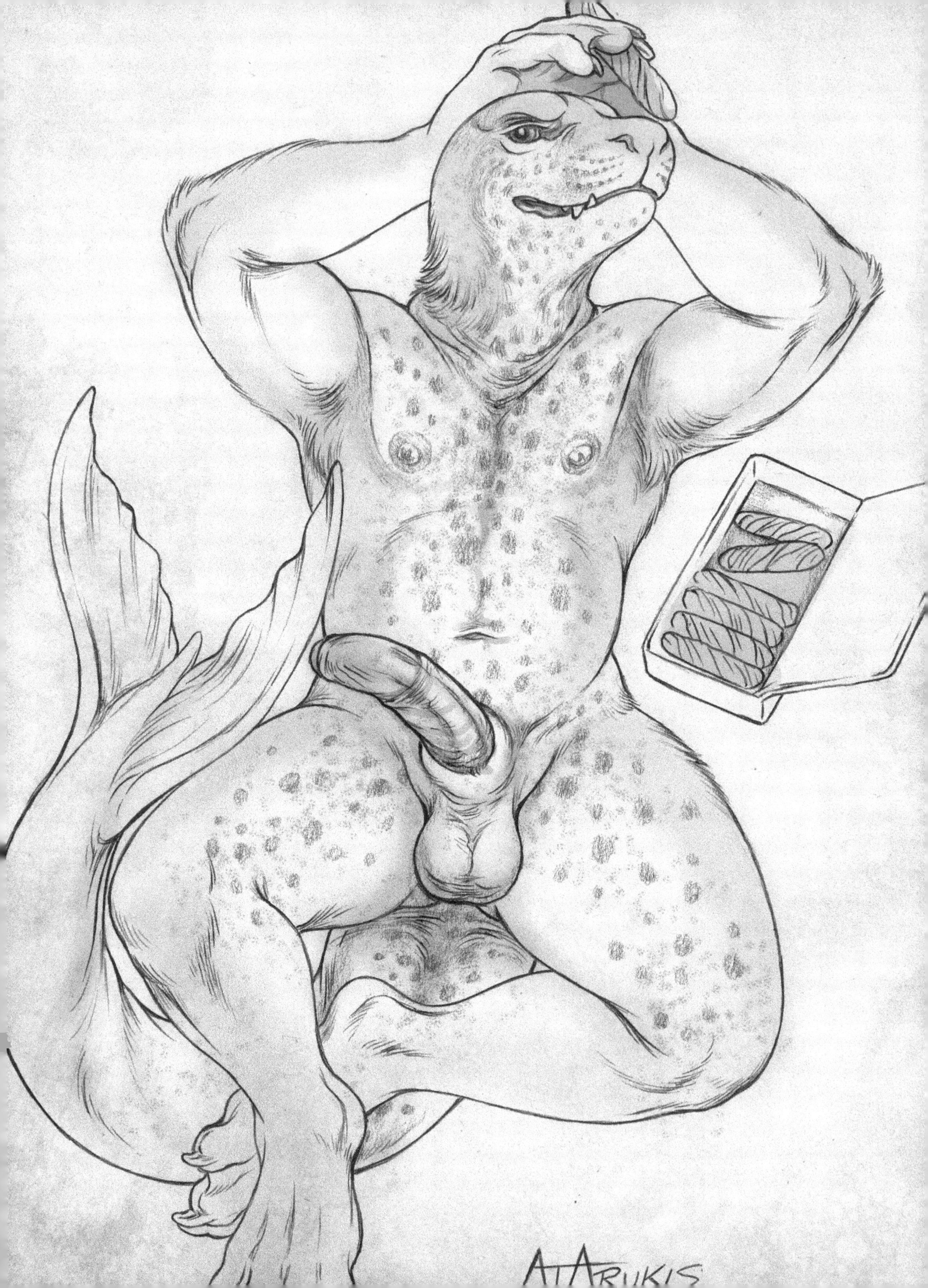

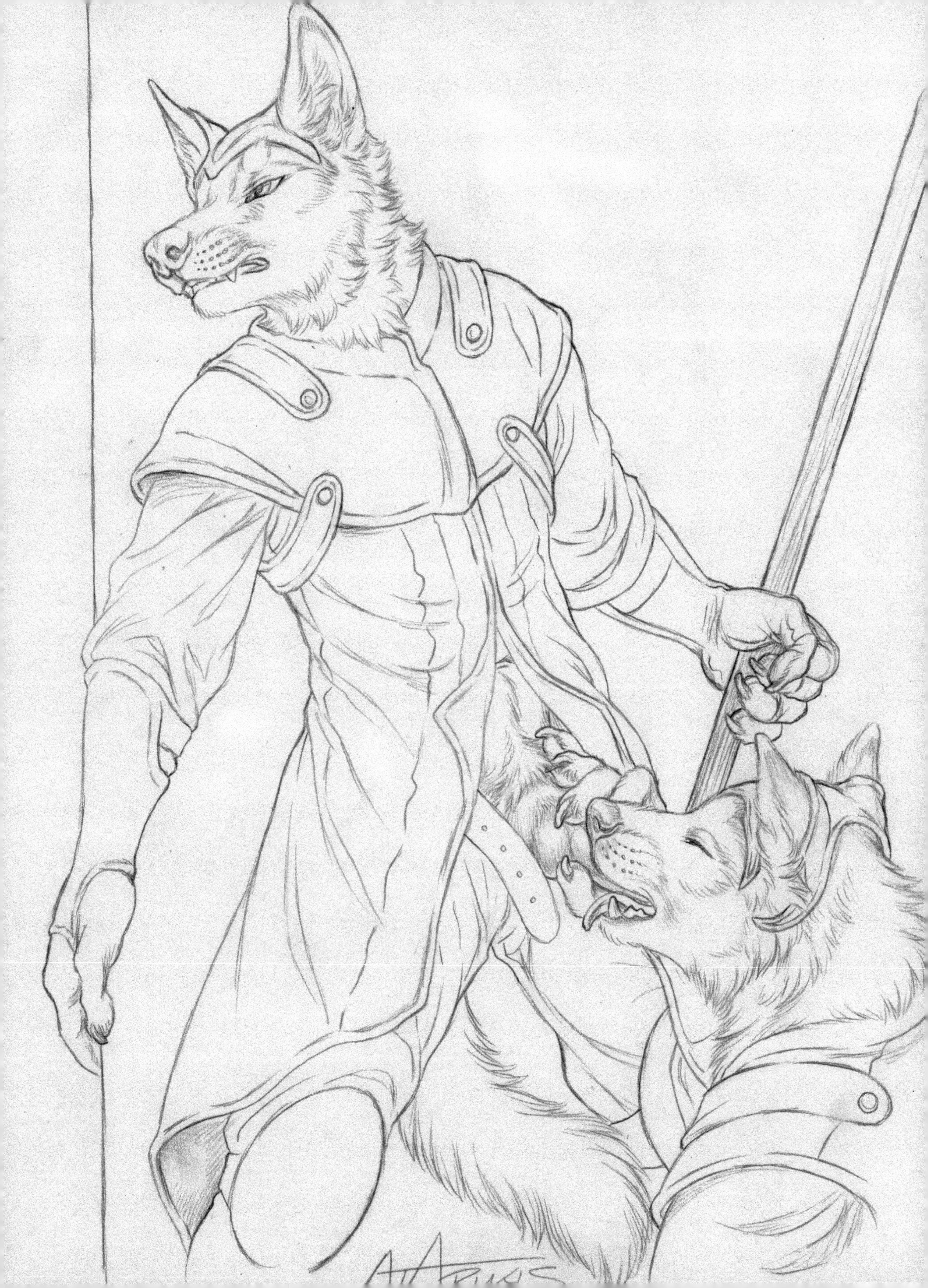

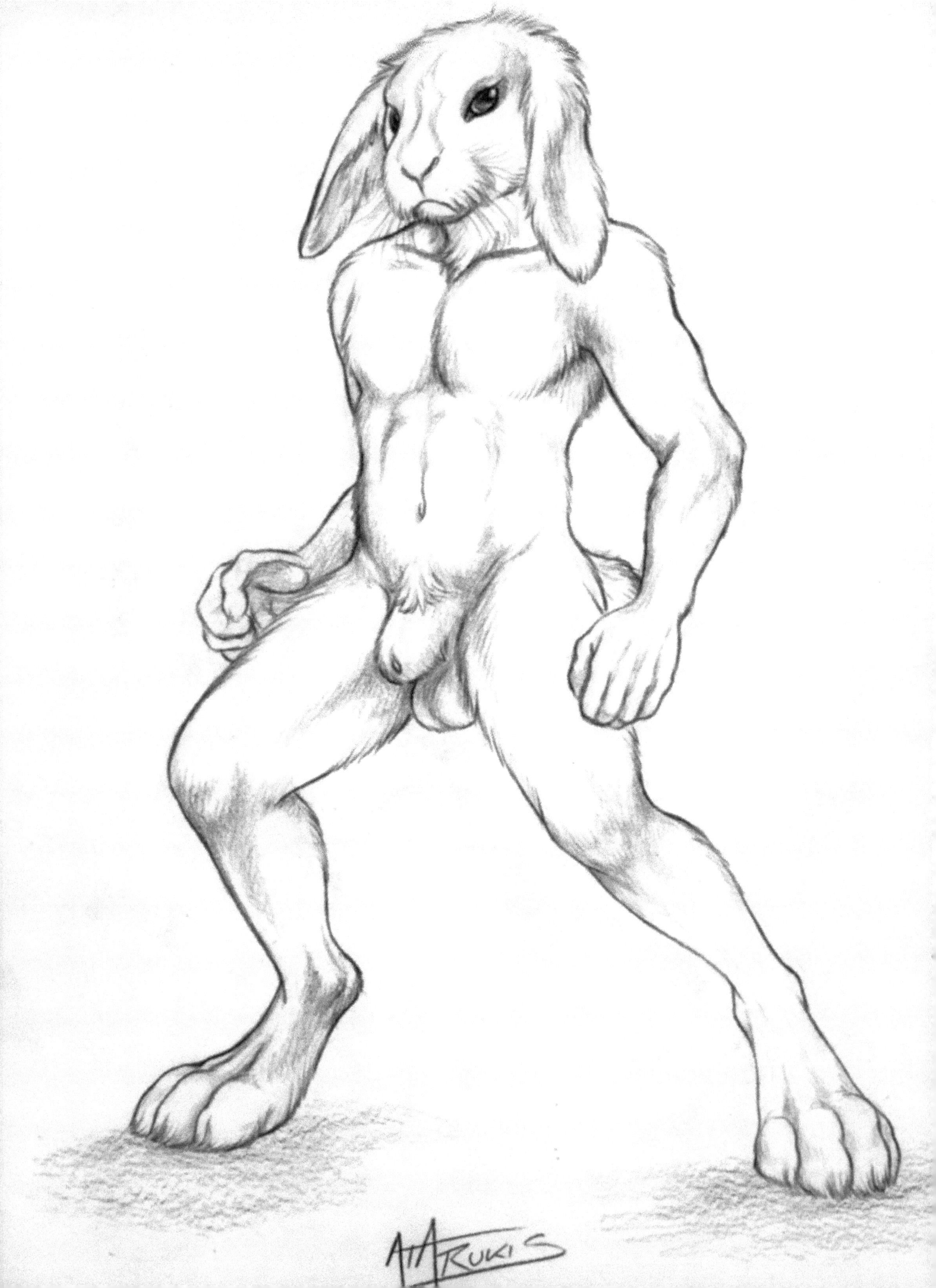

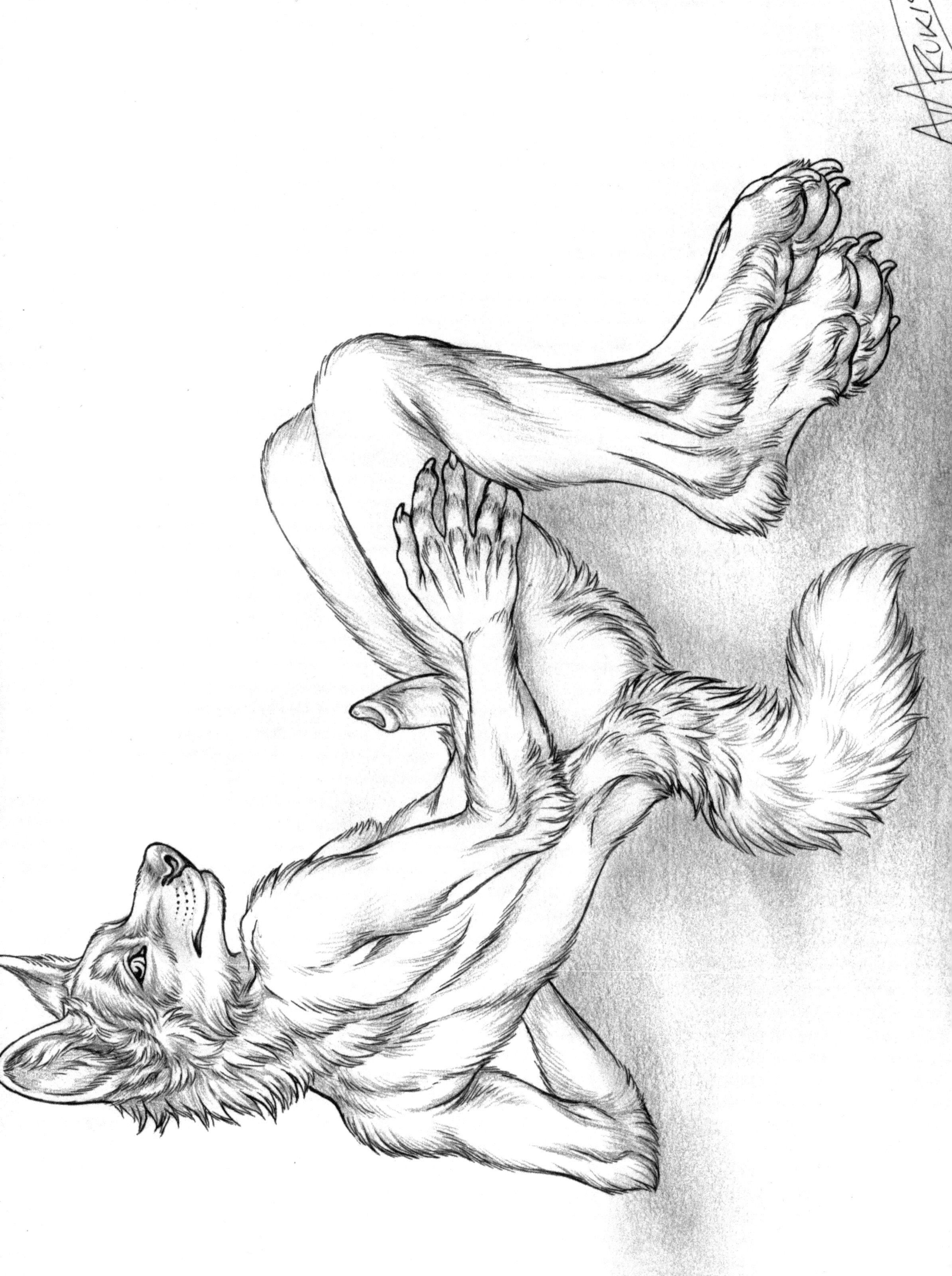

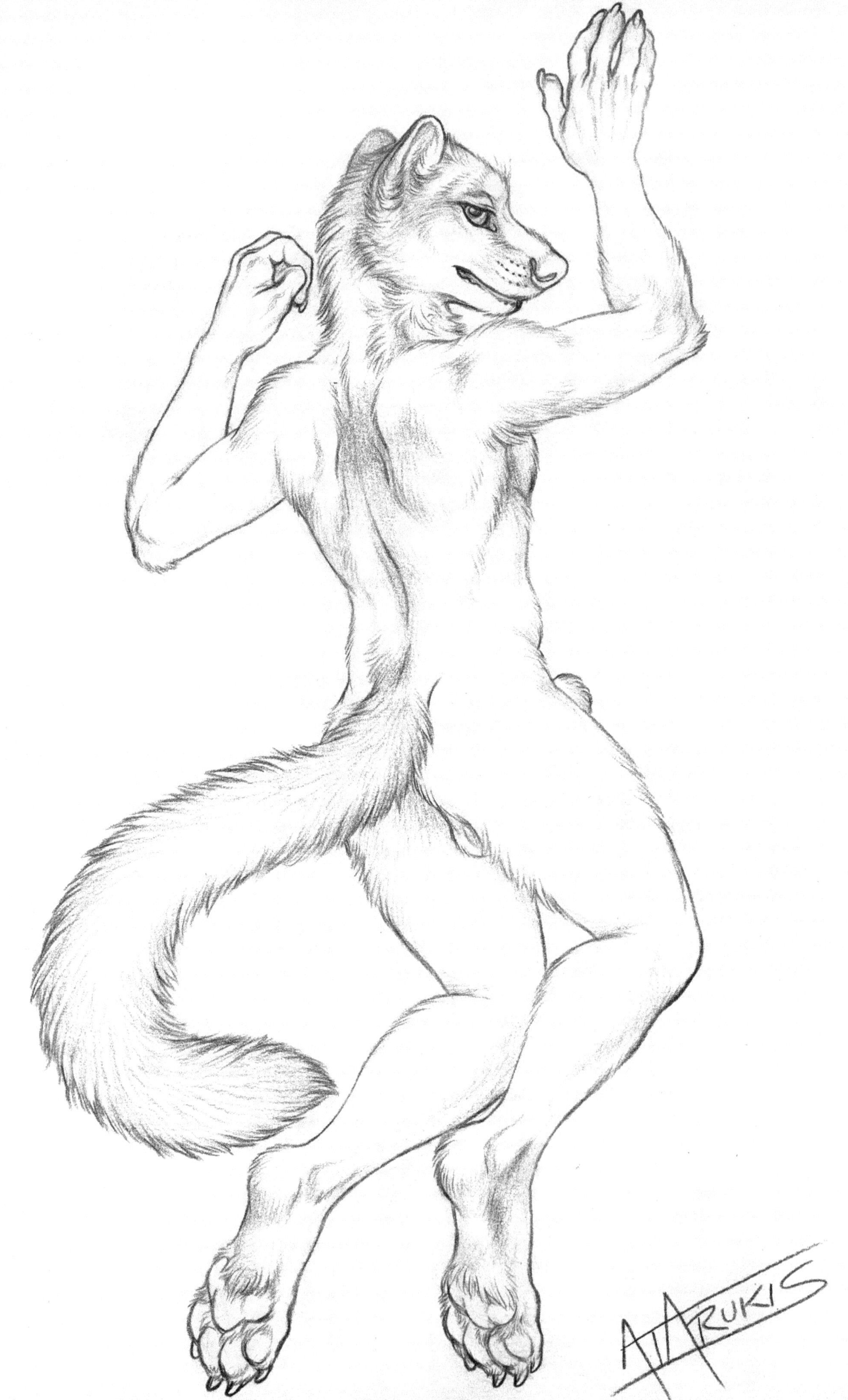

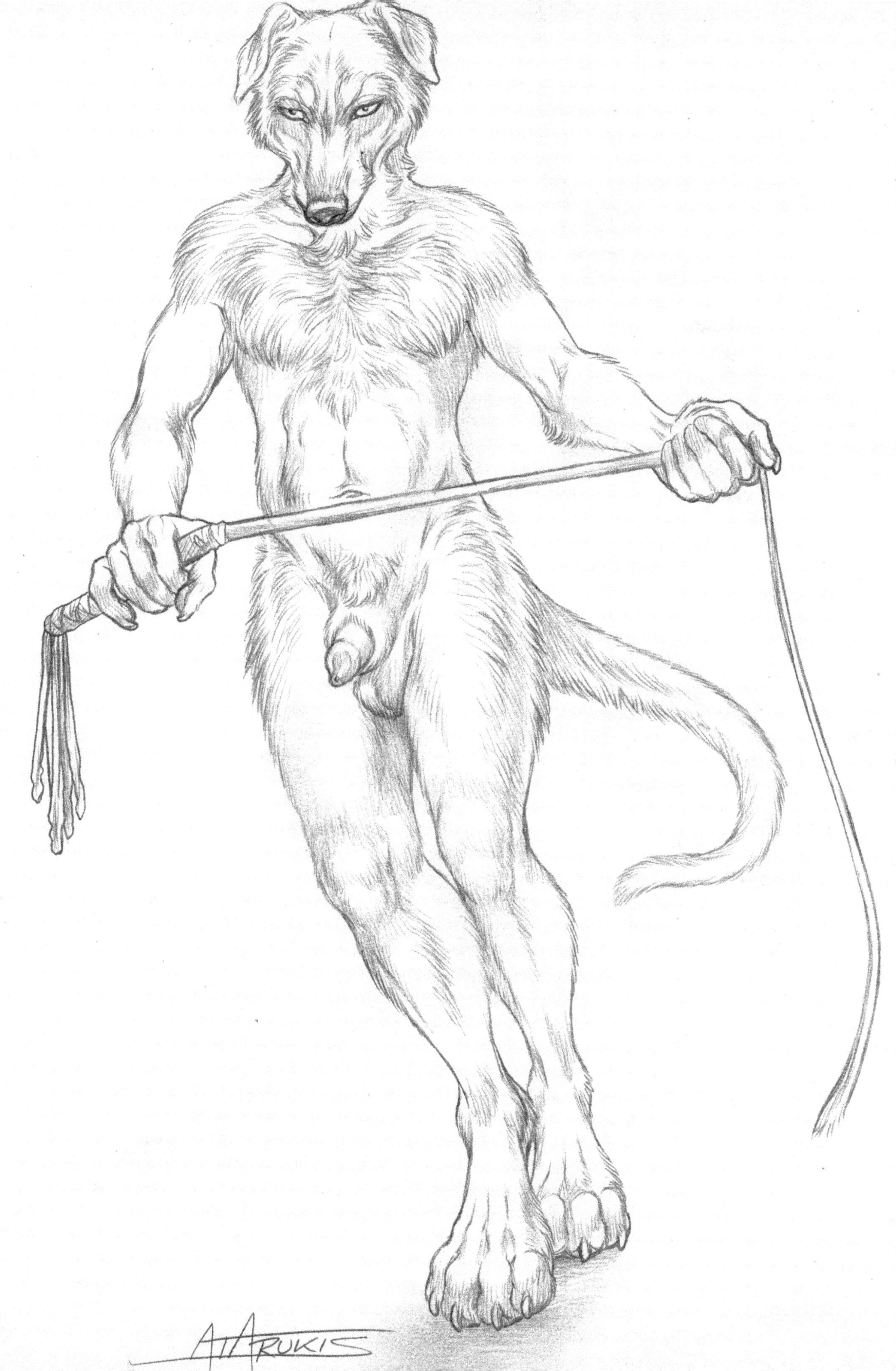

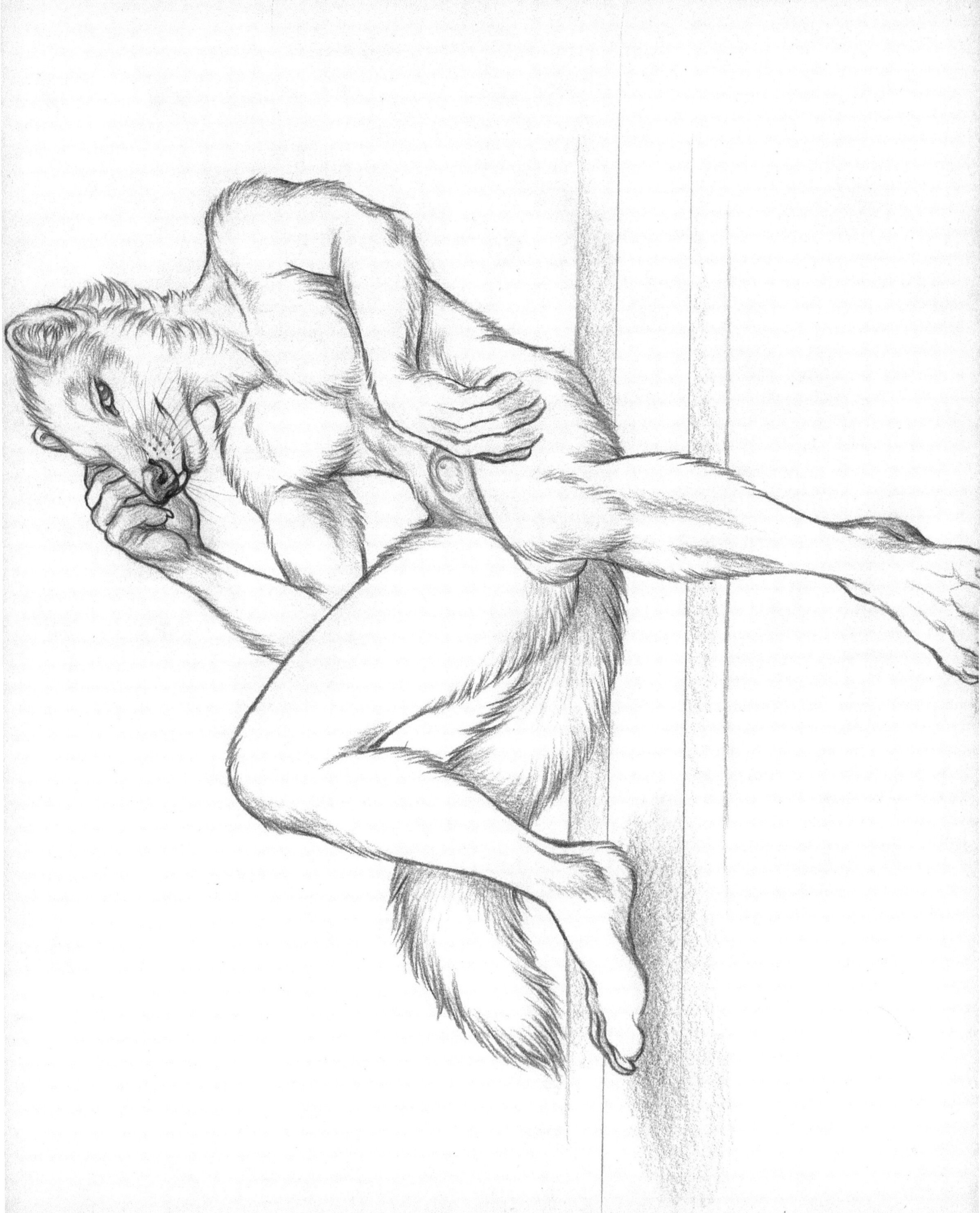

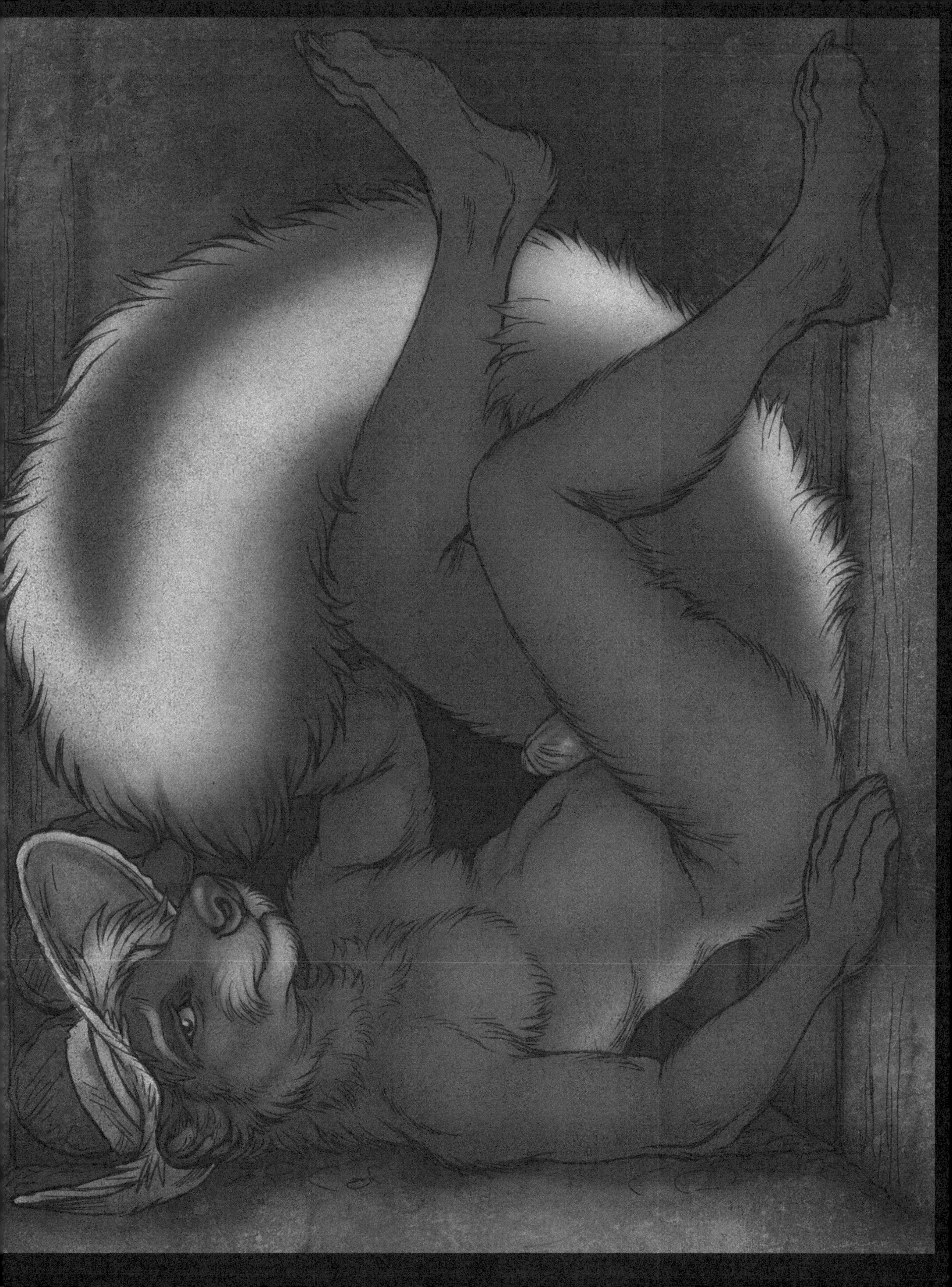

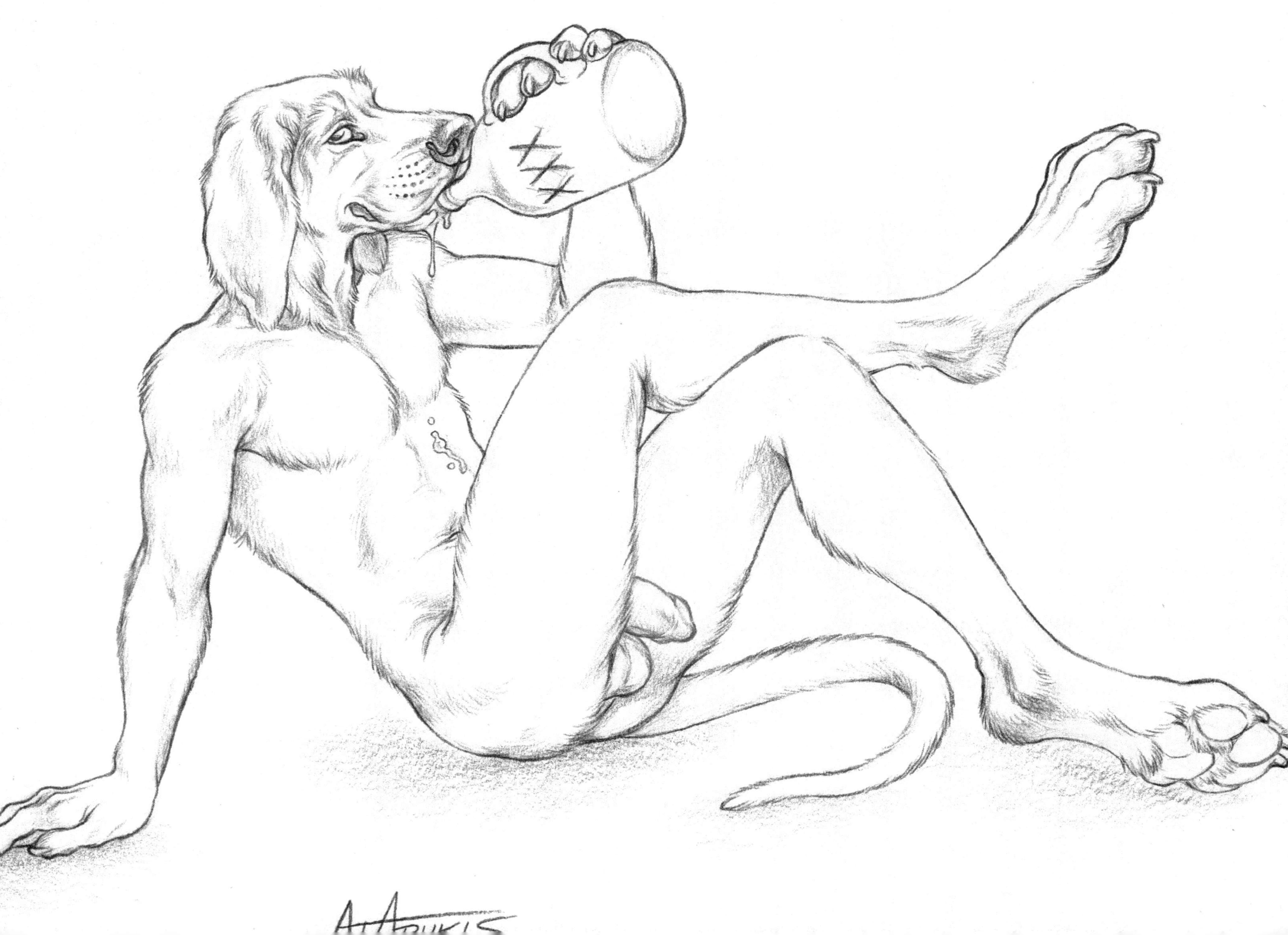

xxx

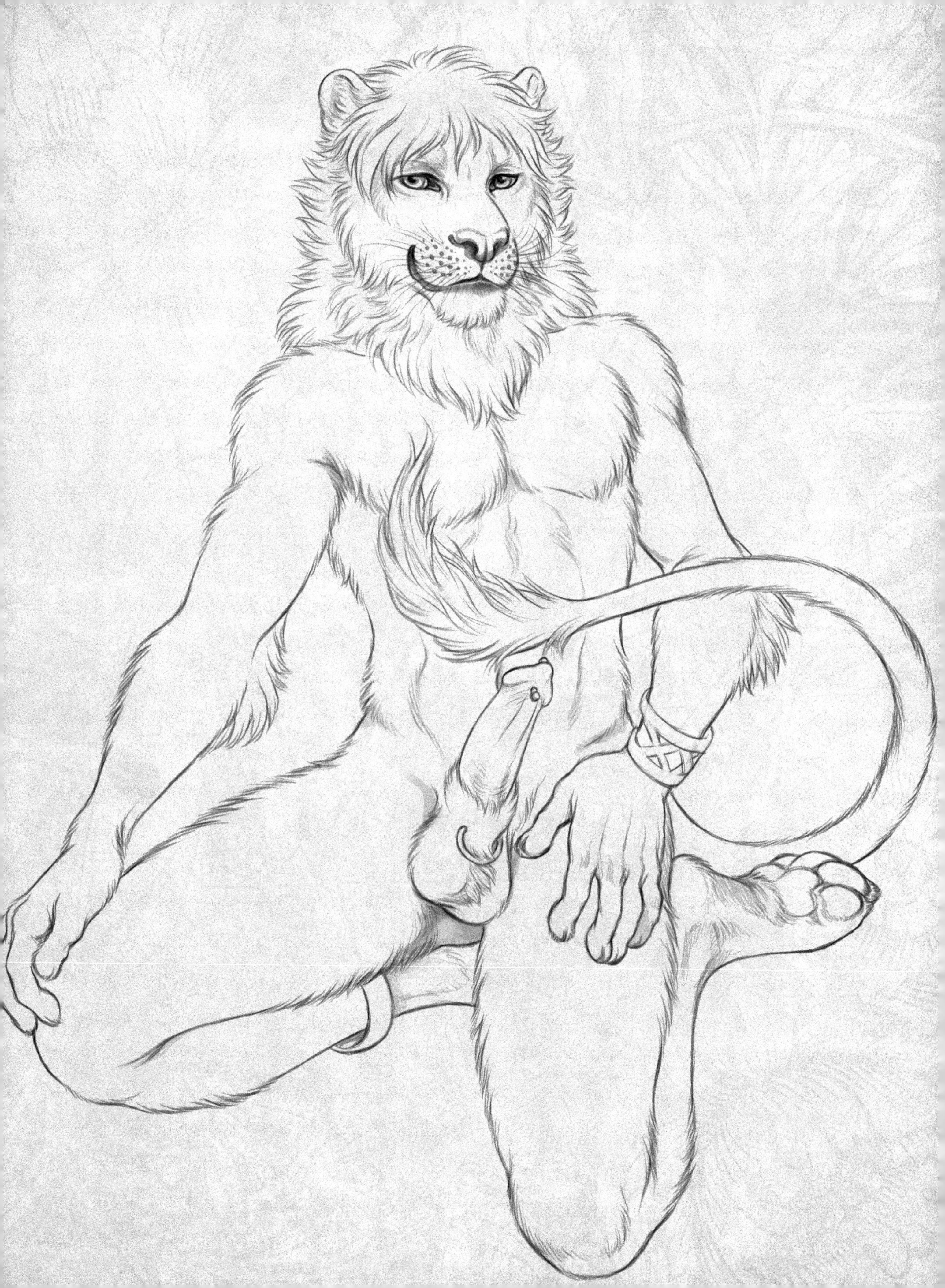

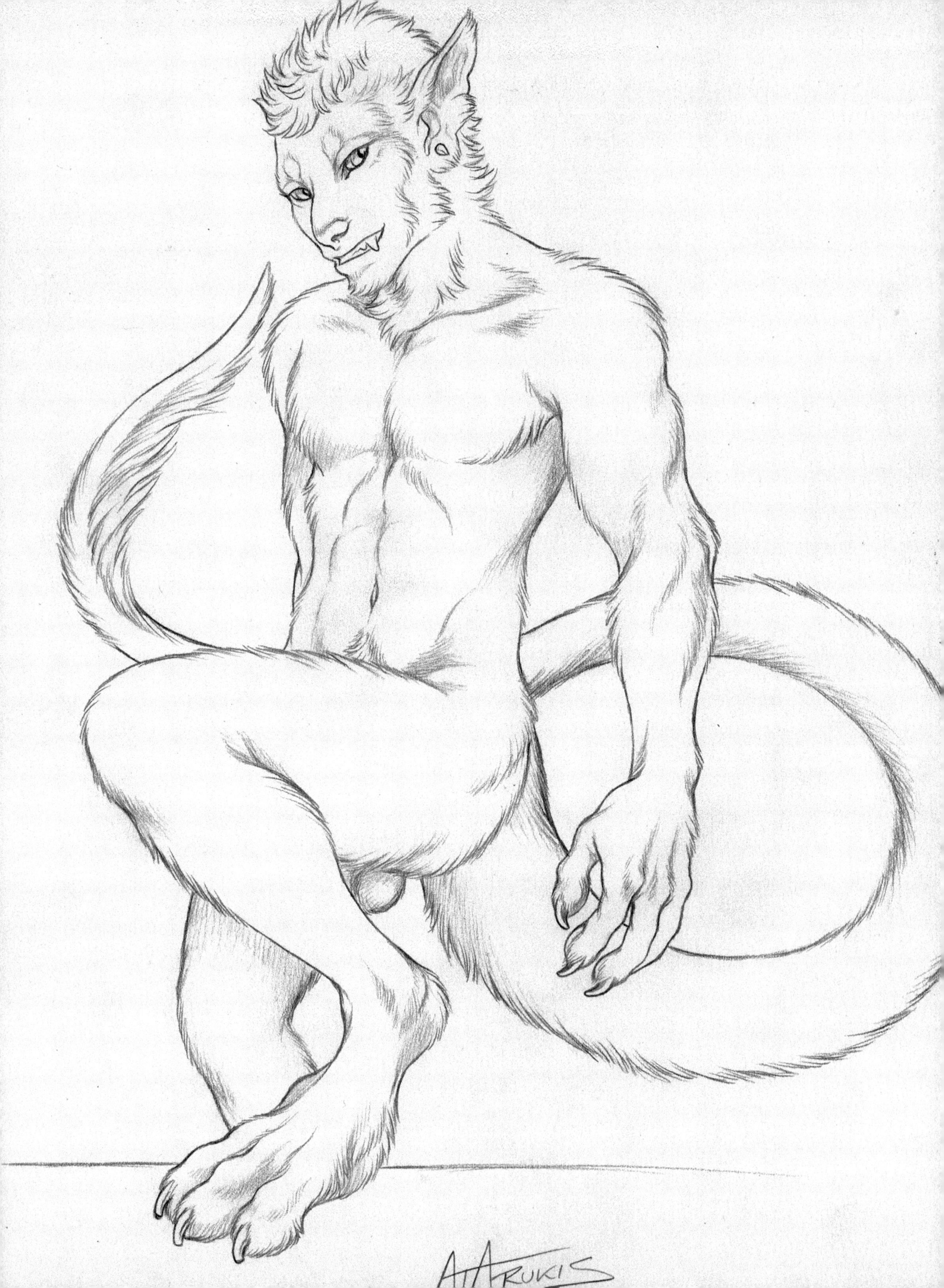

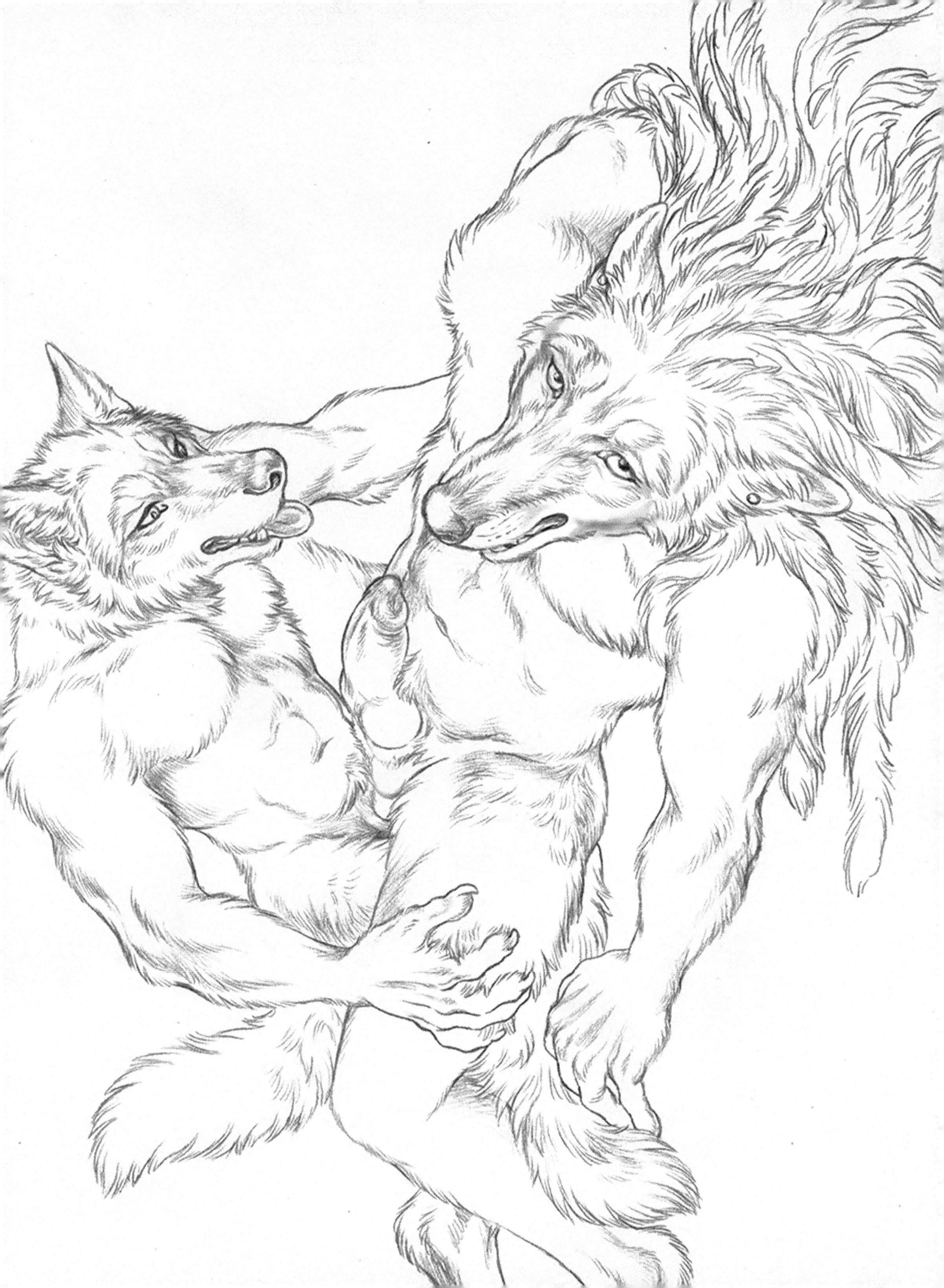

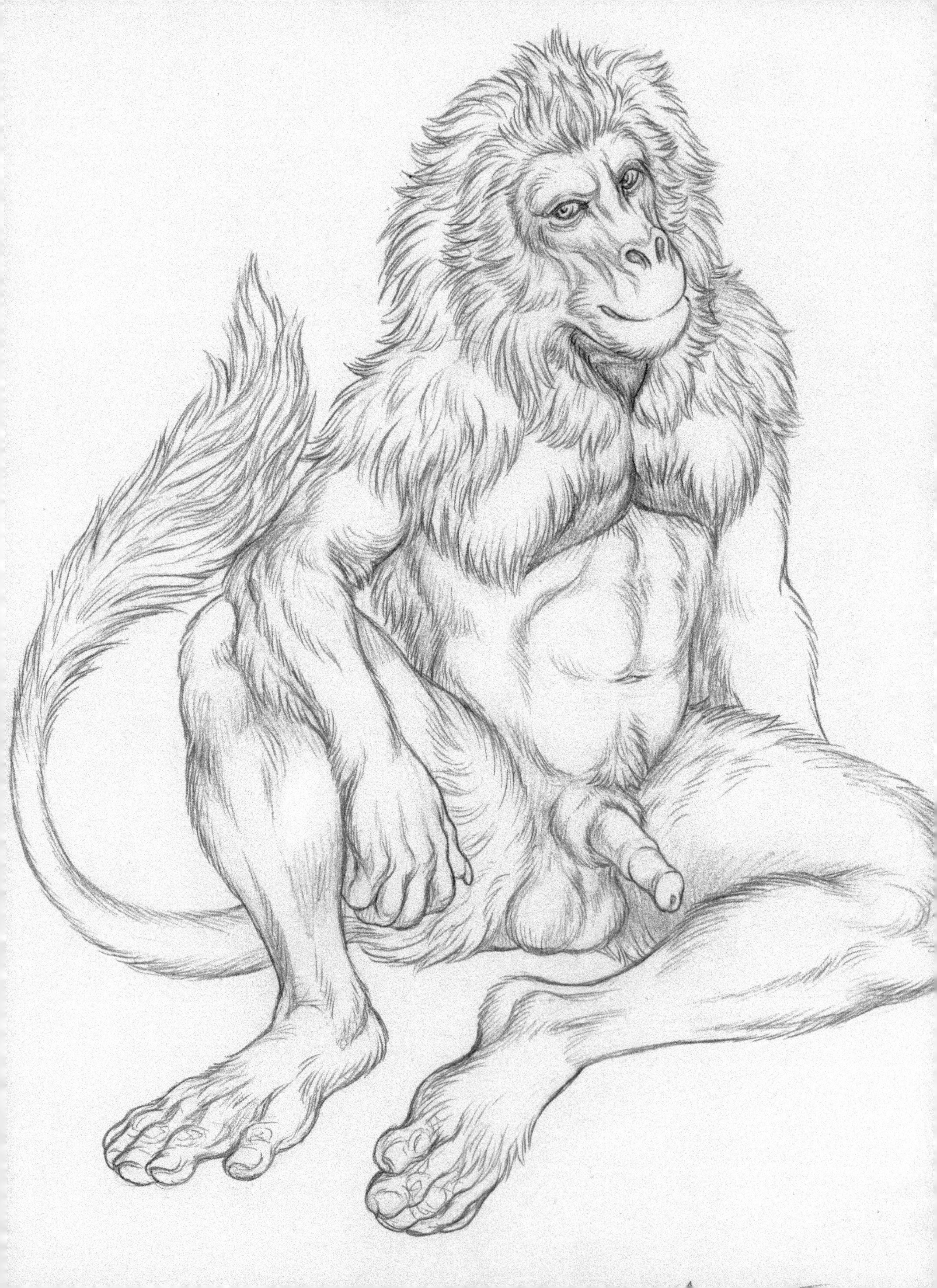

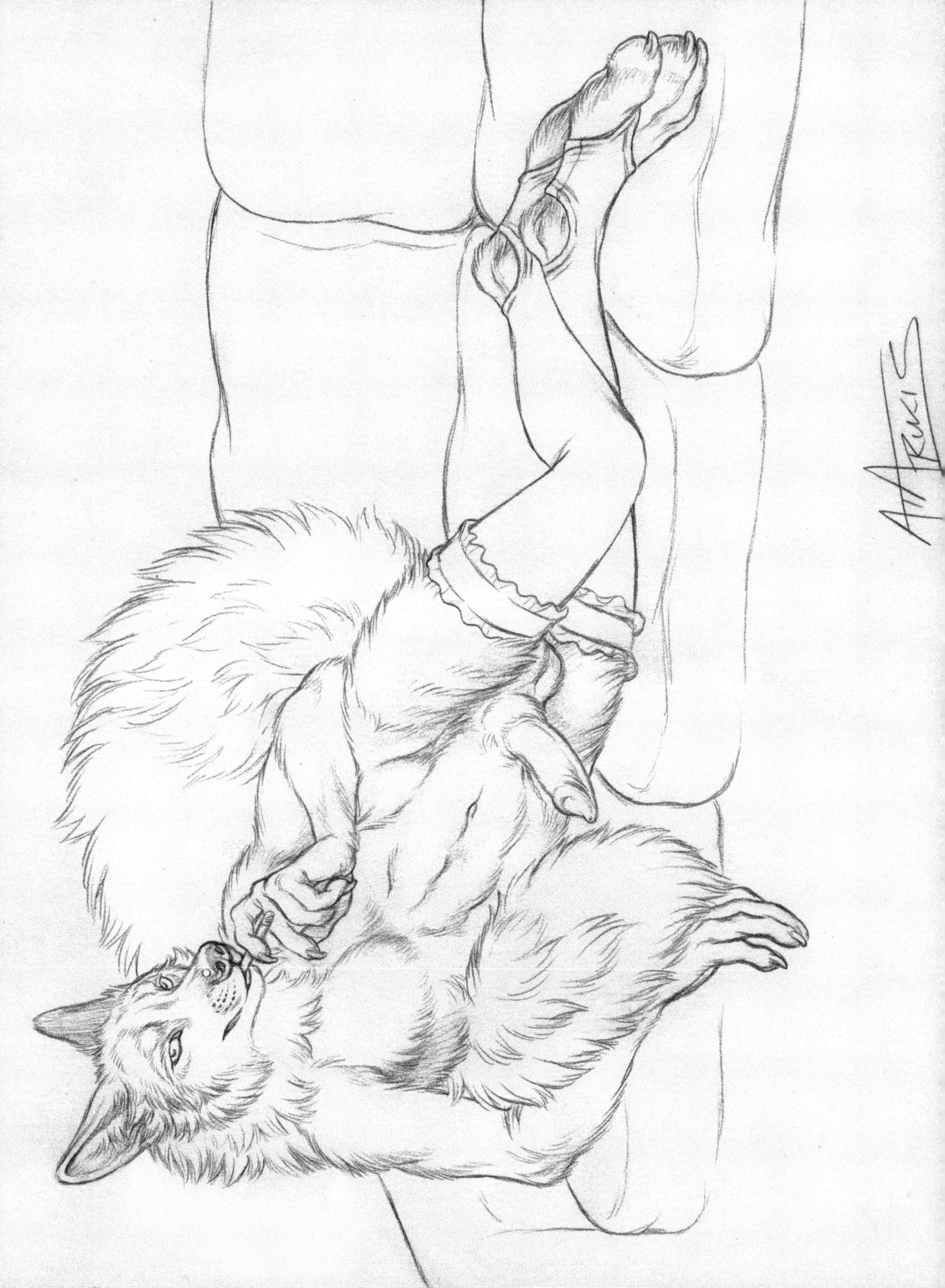

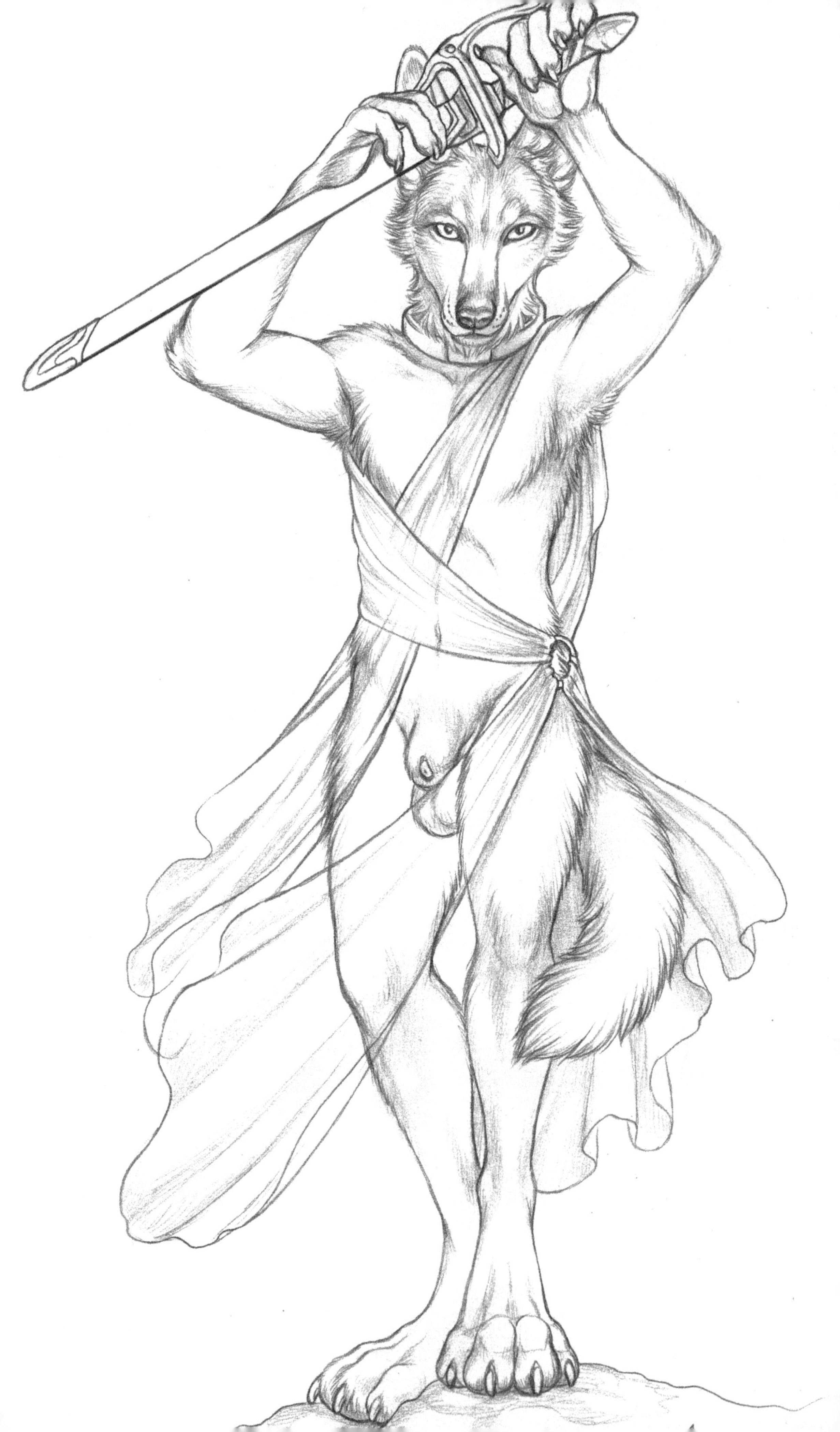

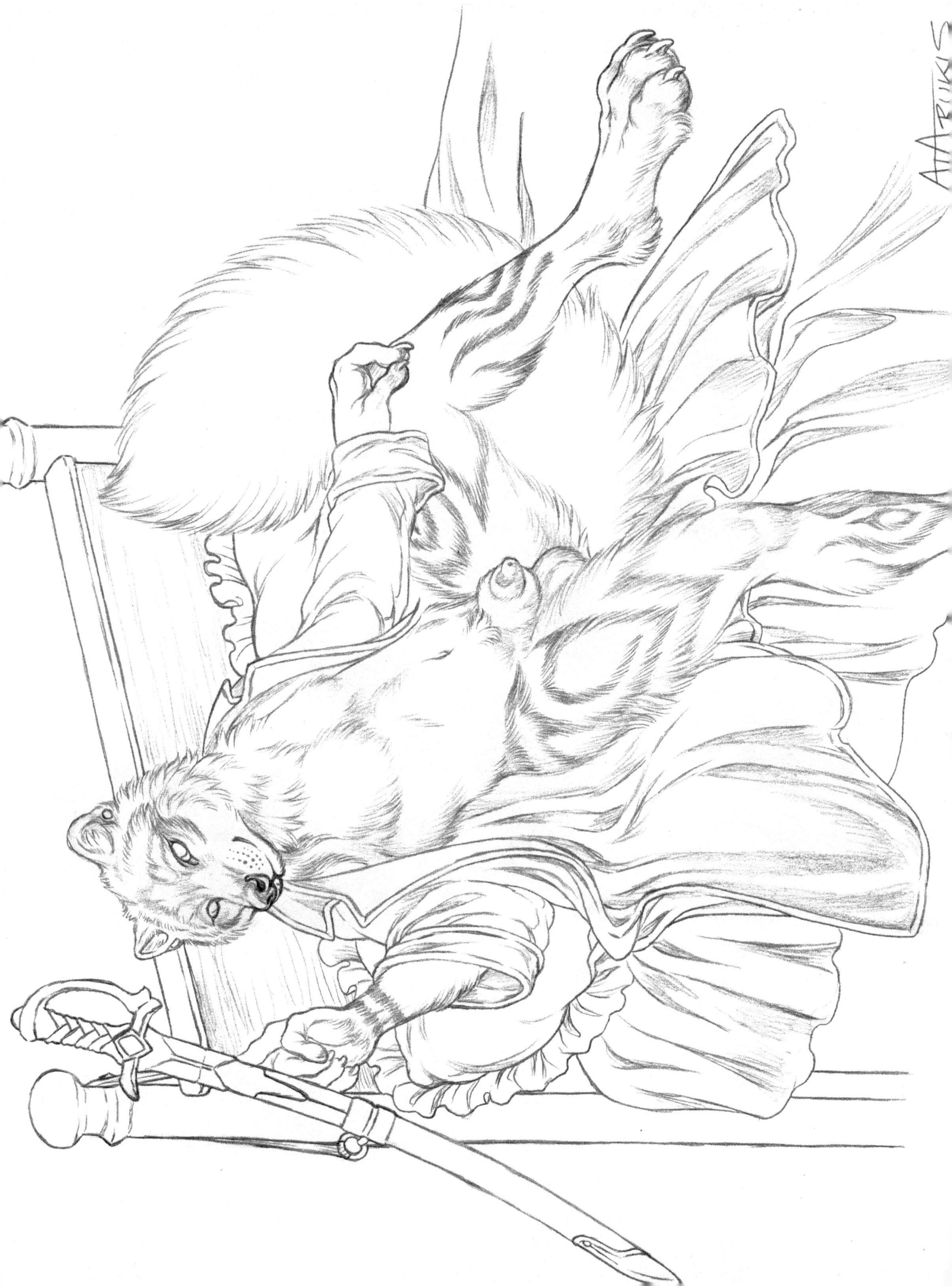

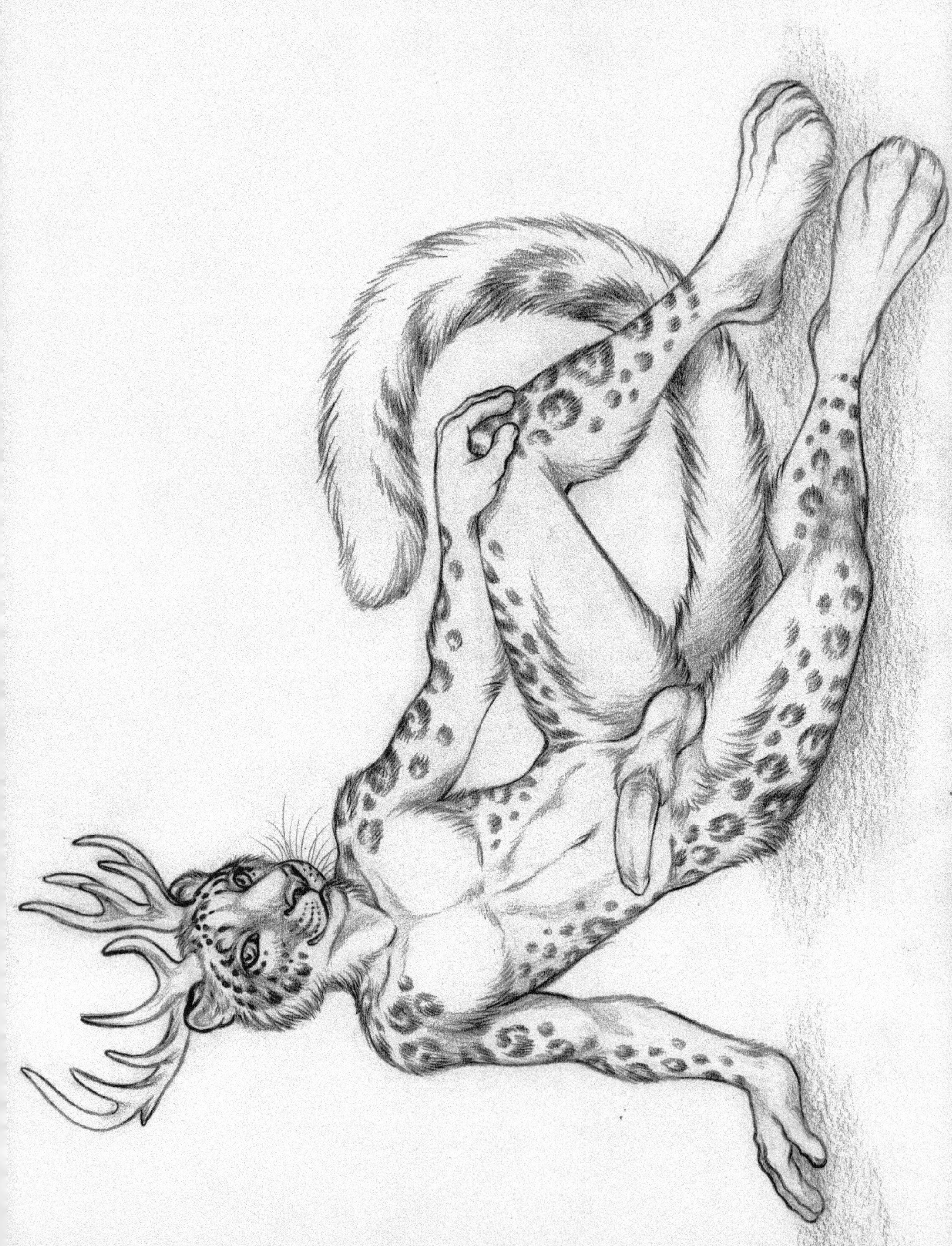

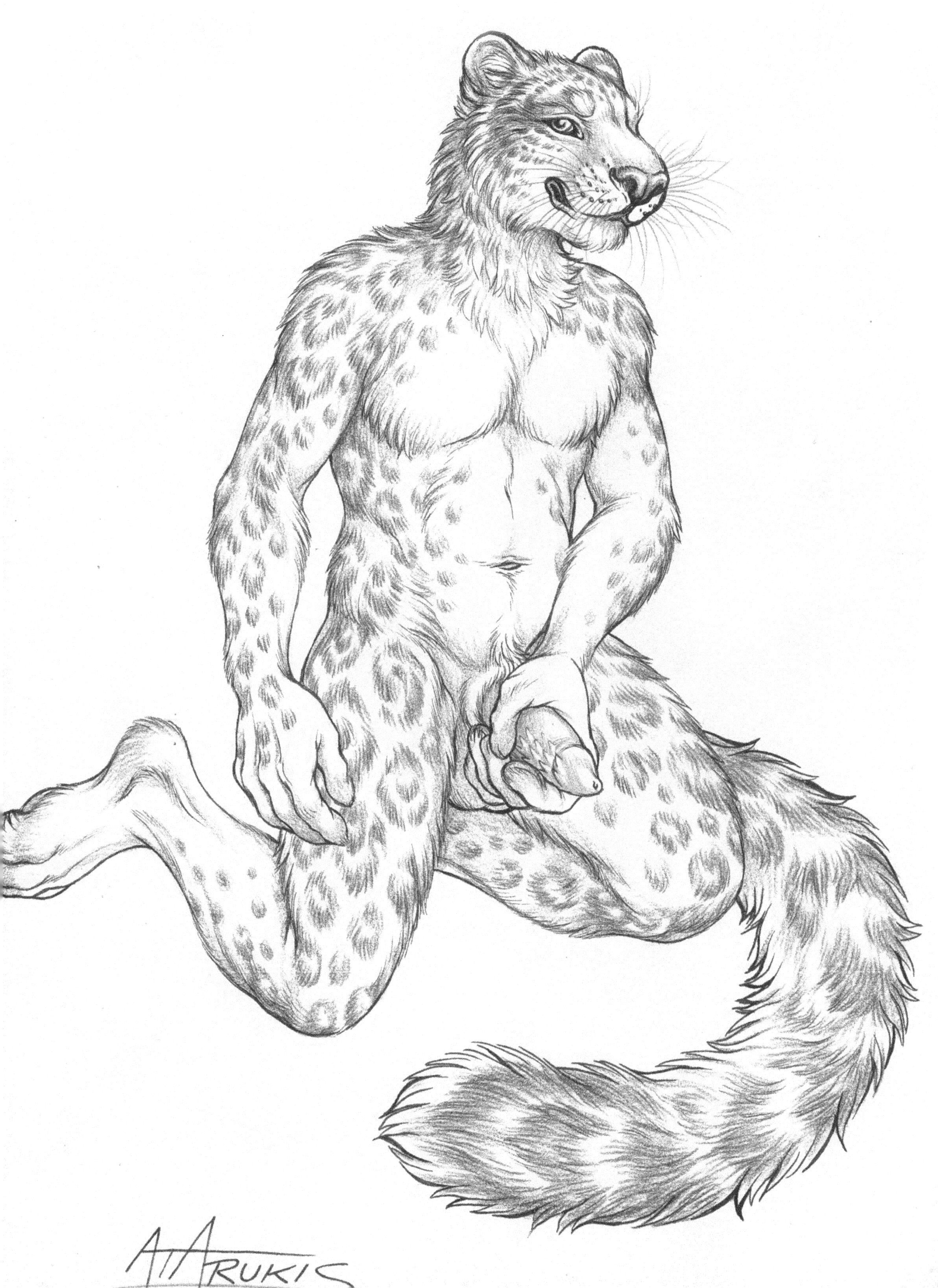
Arukis

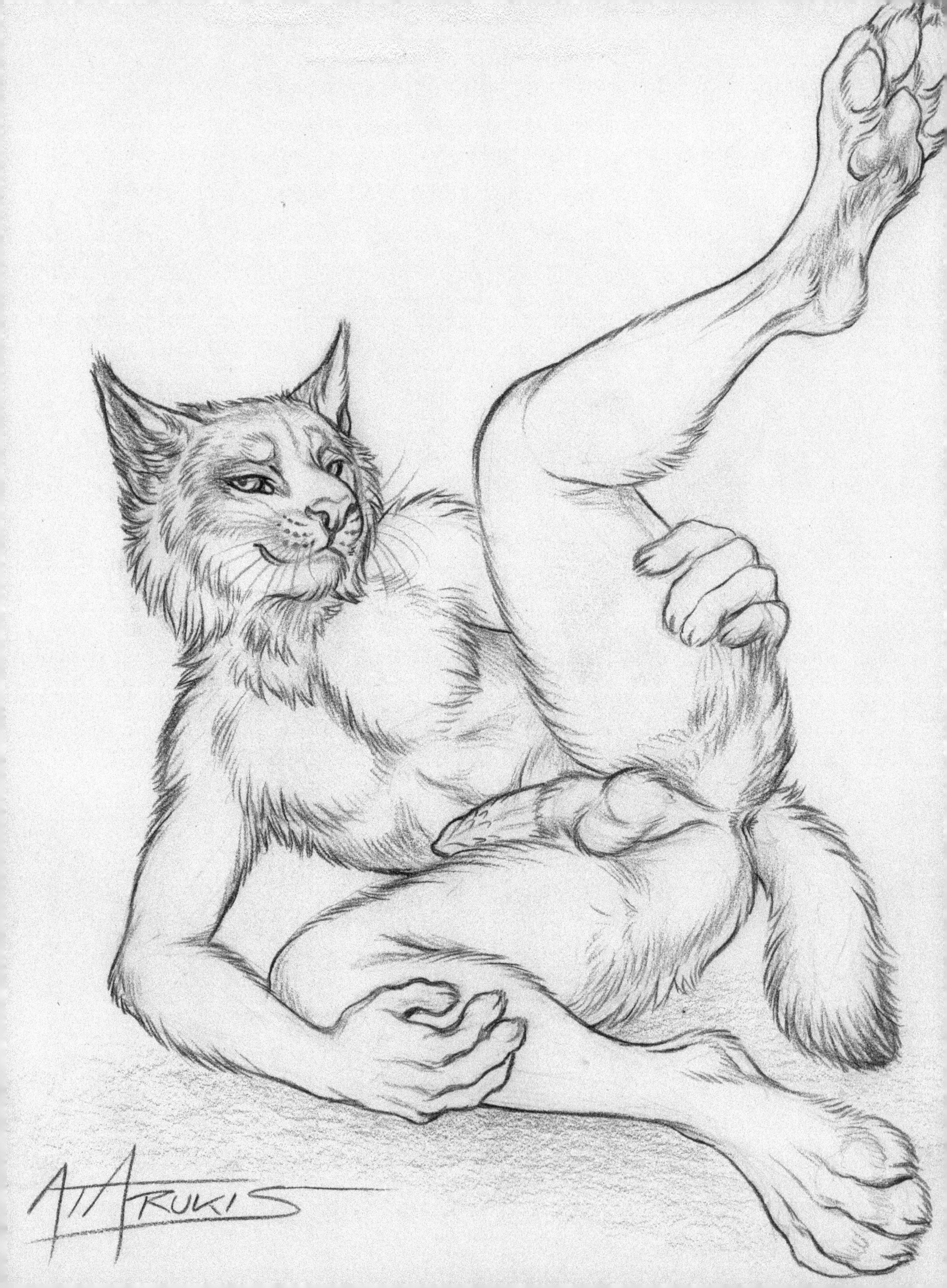

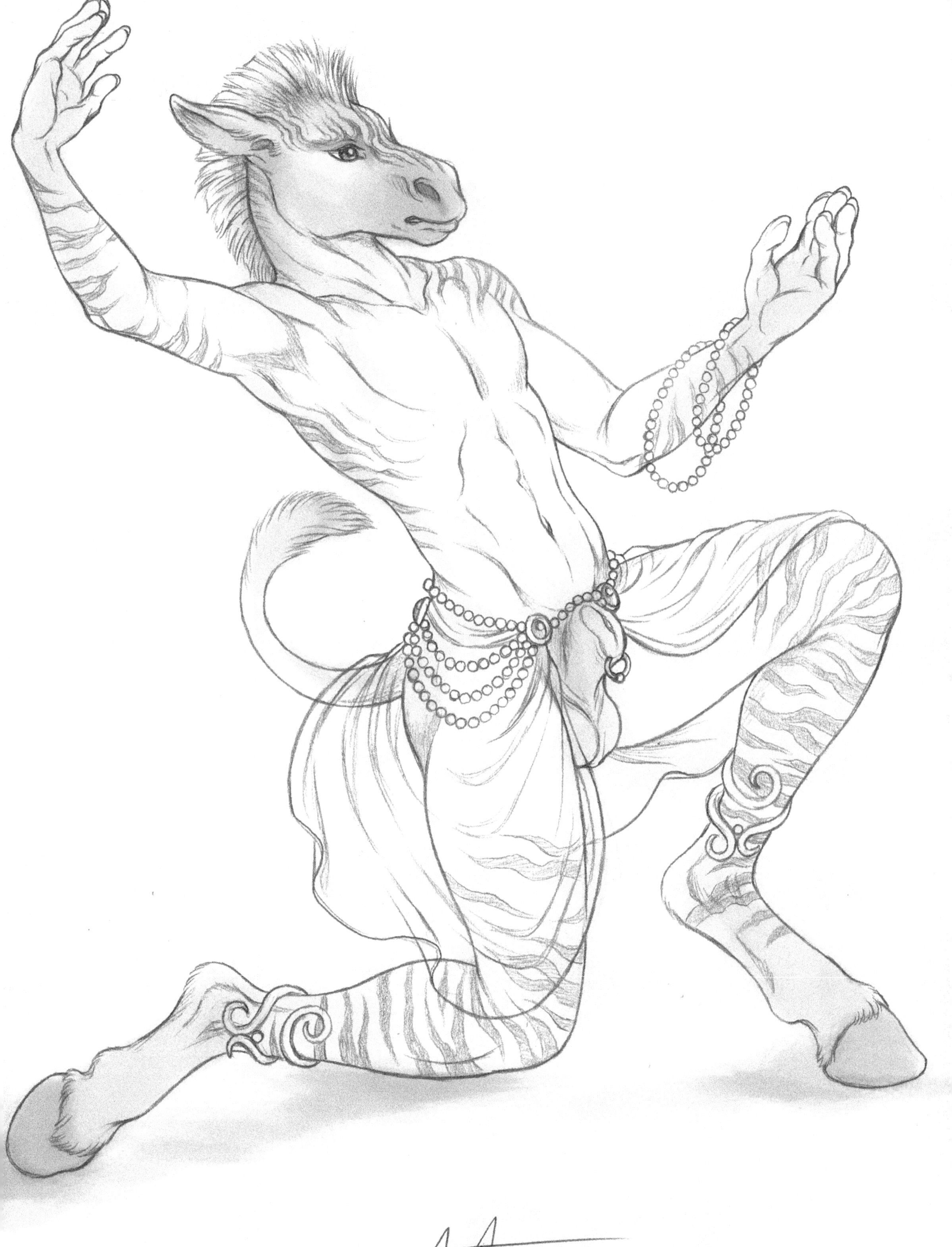

A!Arukis

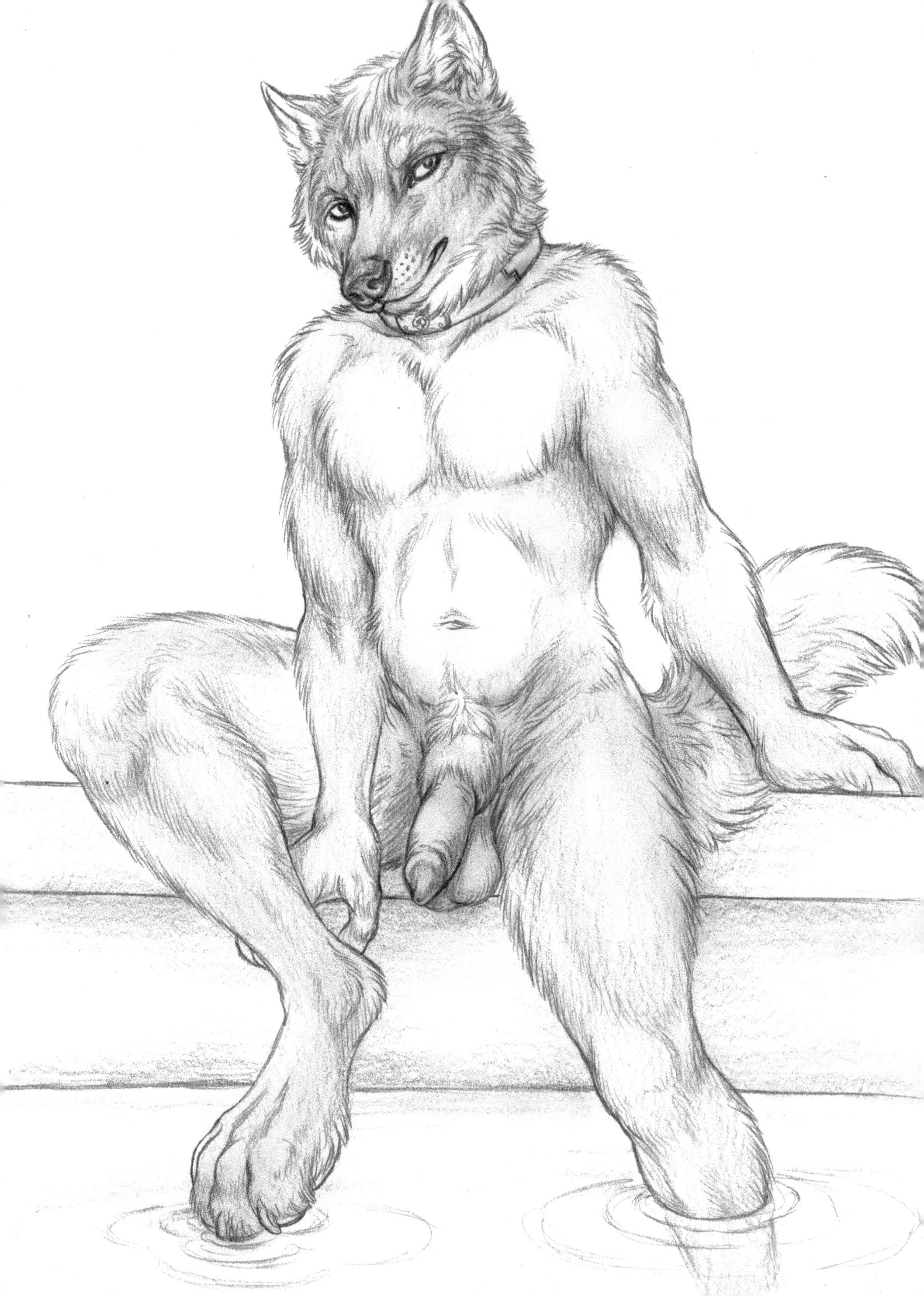

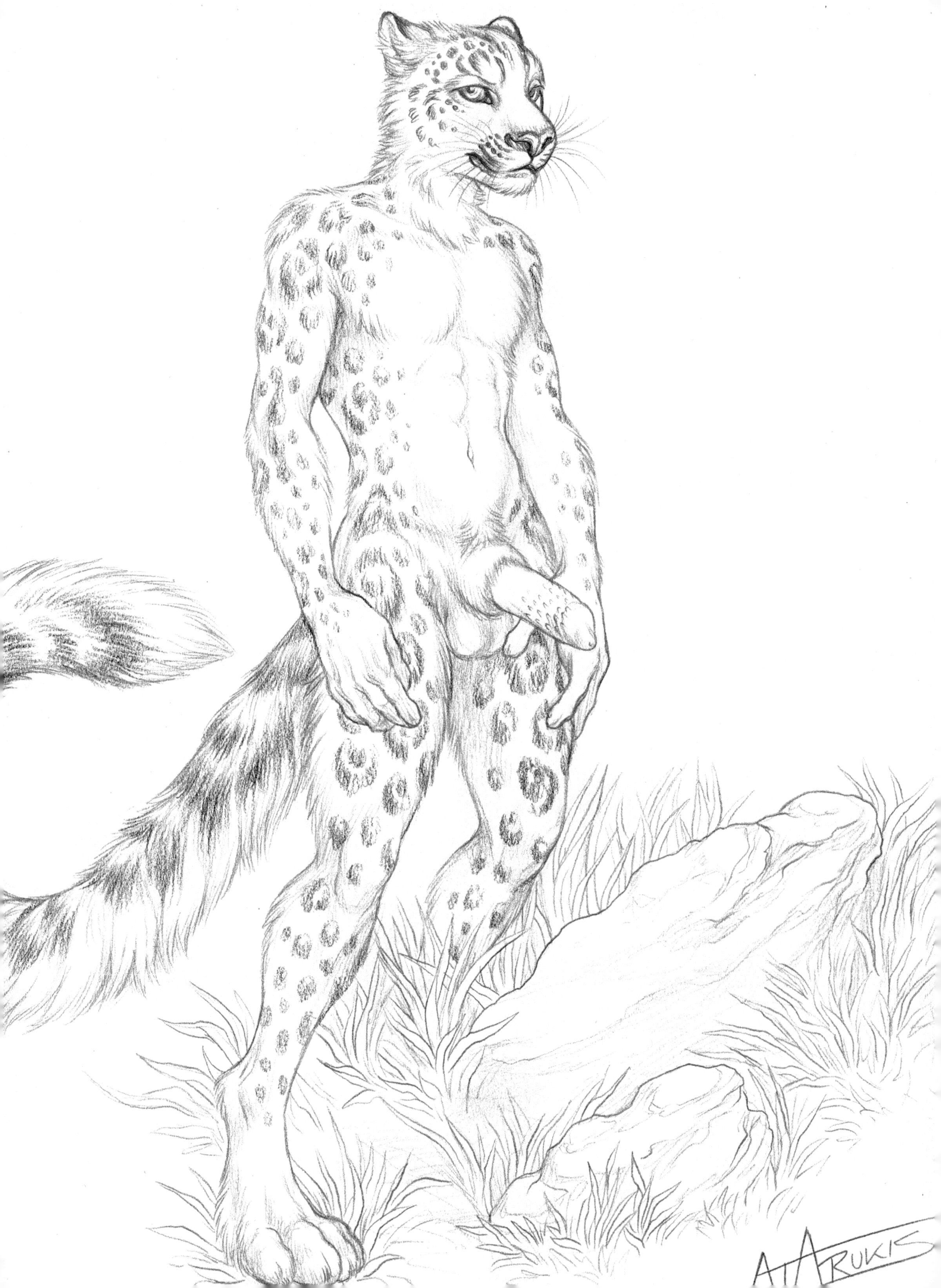

AT ARUKIS

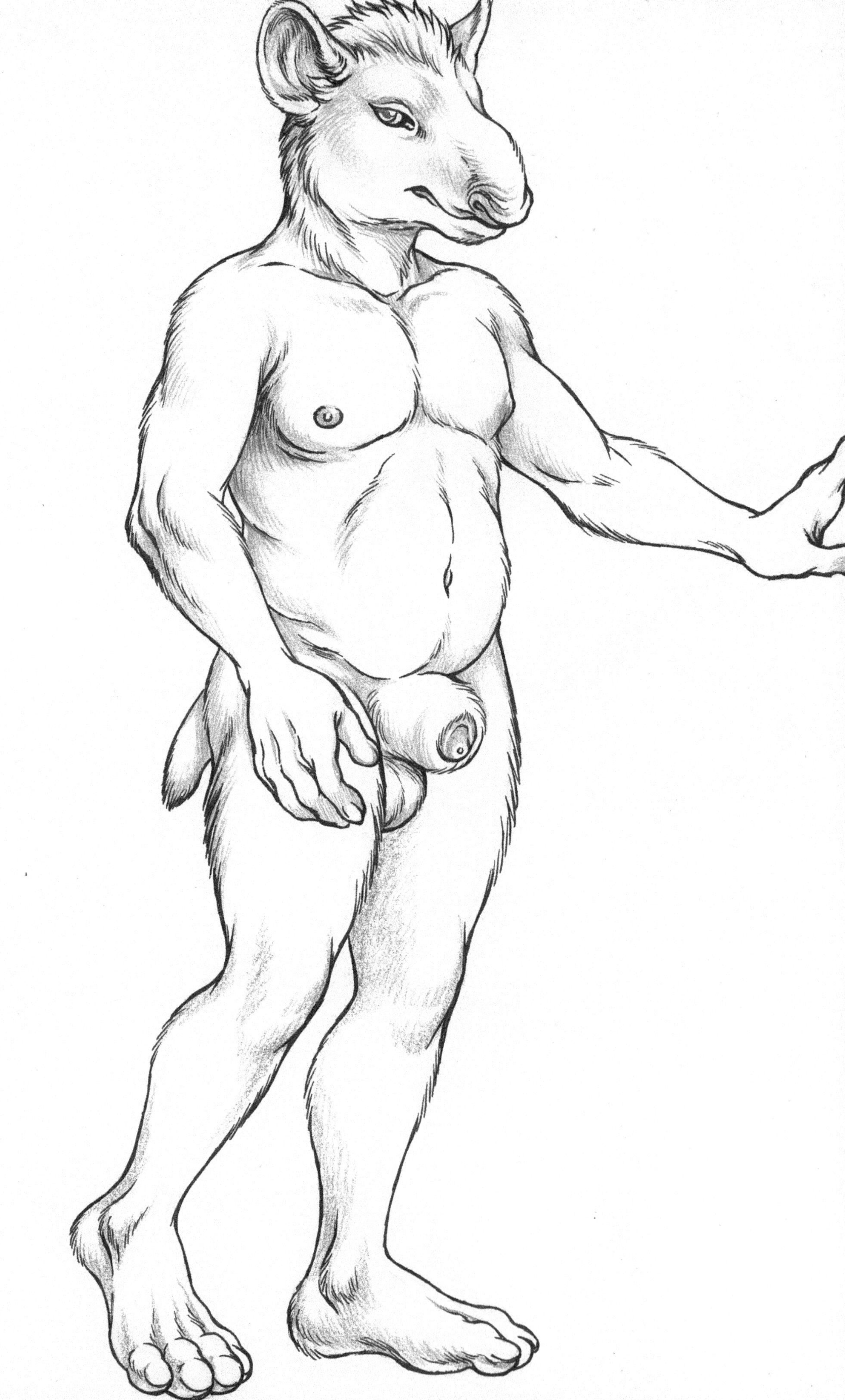

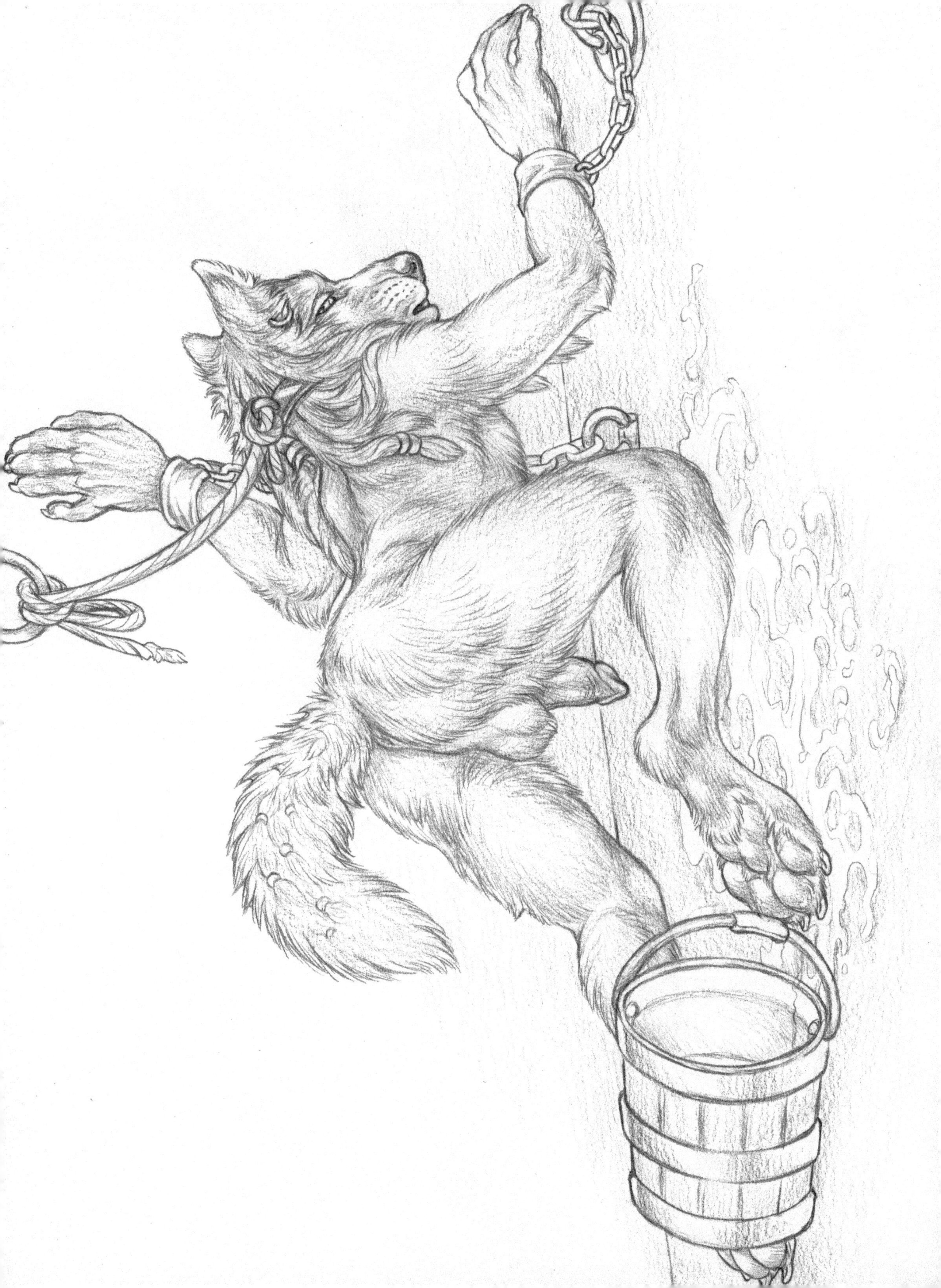

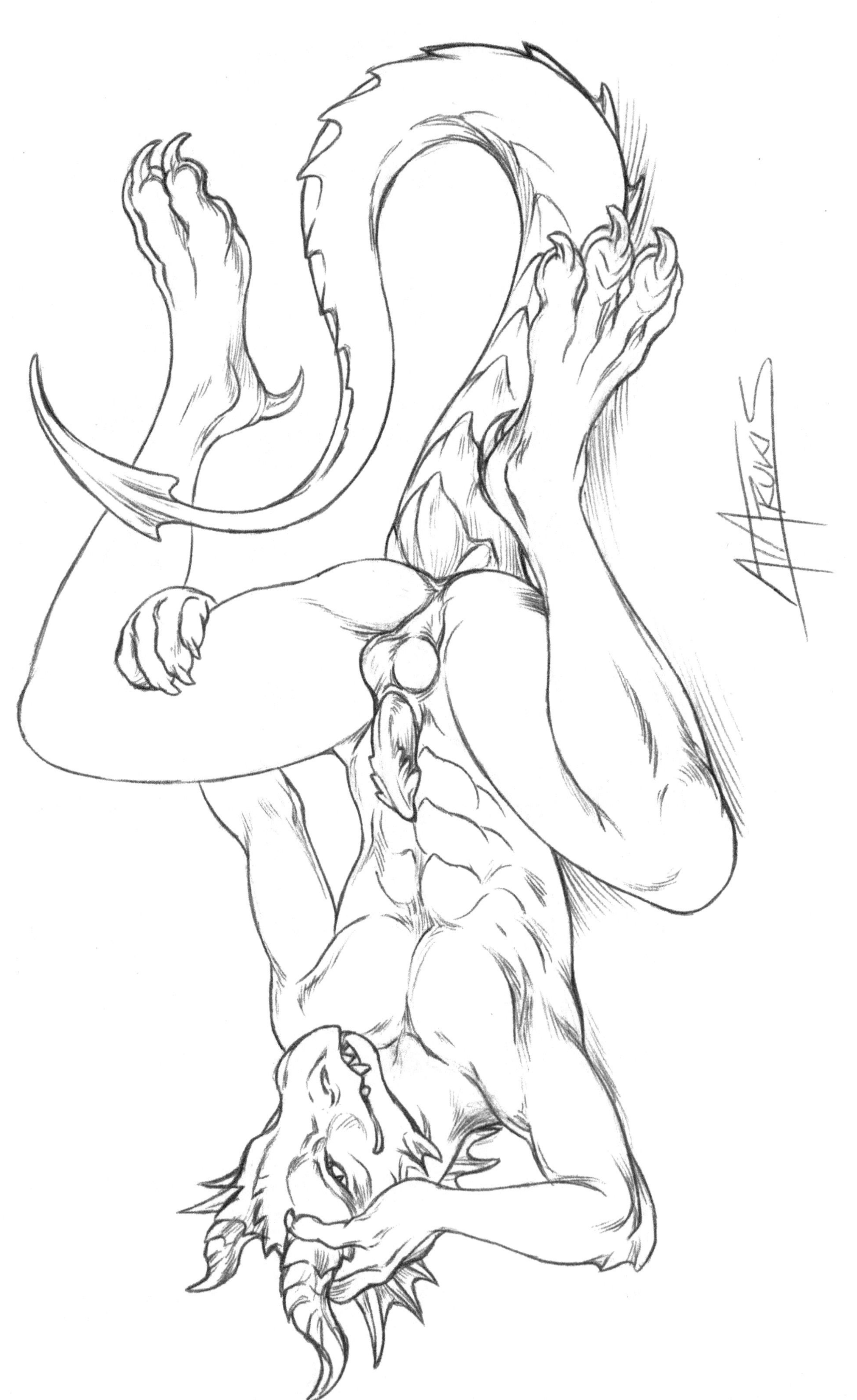

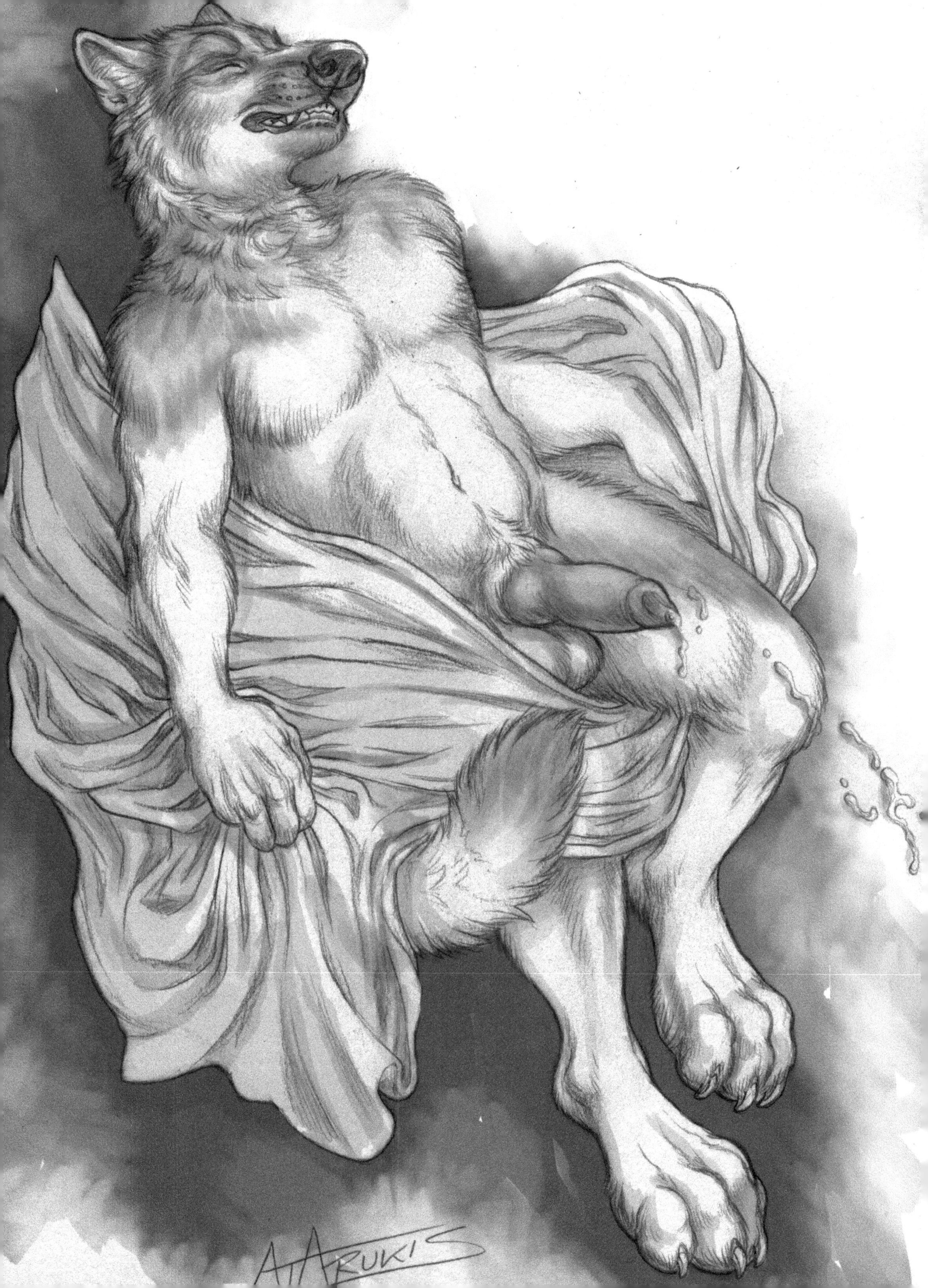
ARUKIS

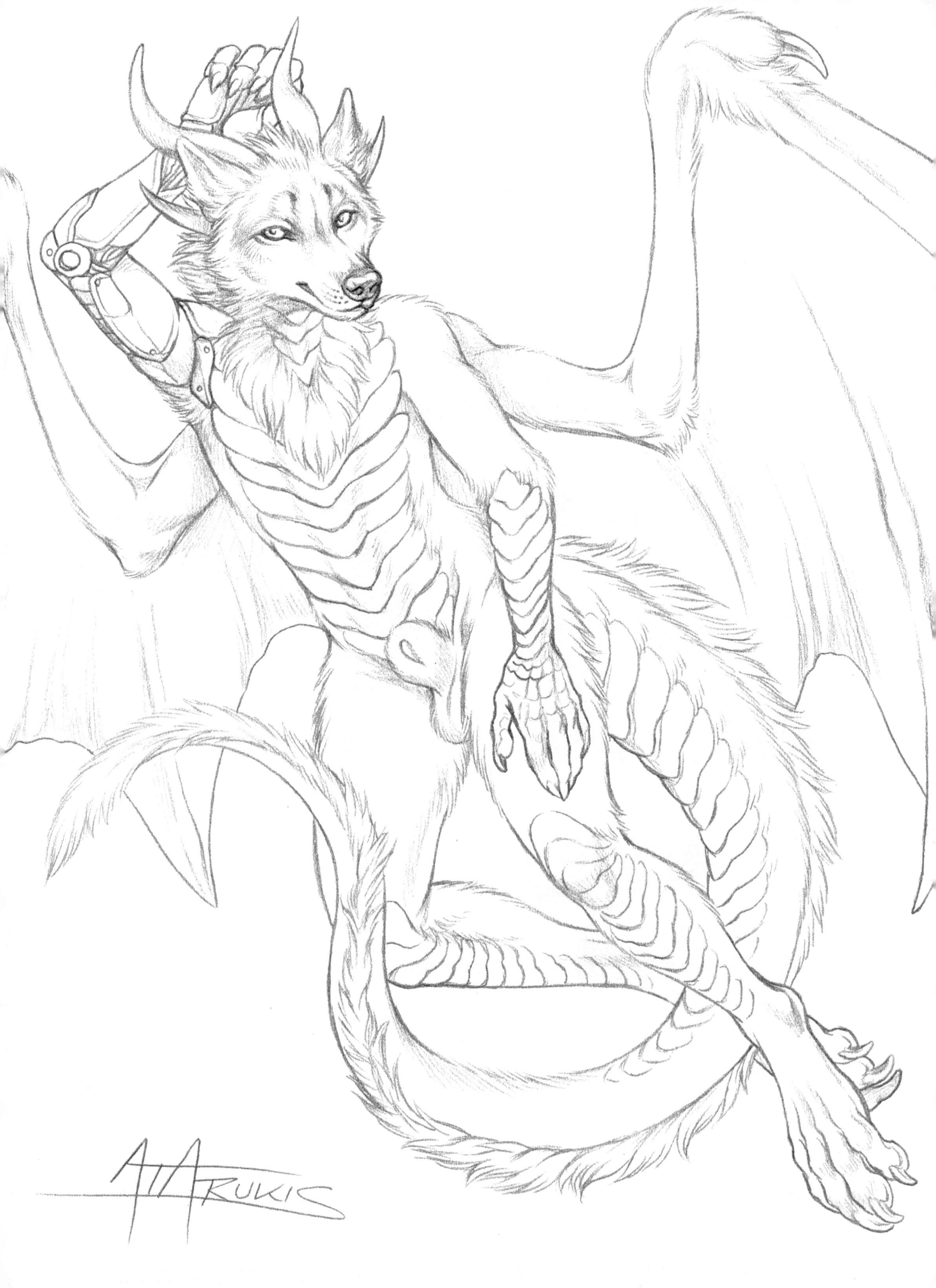

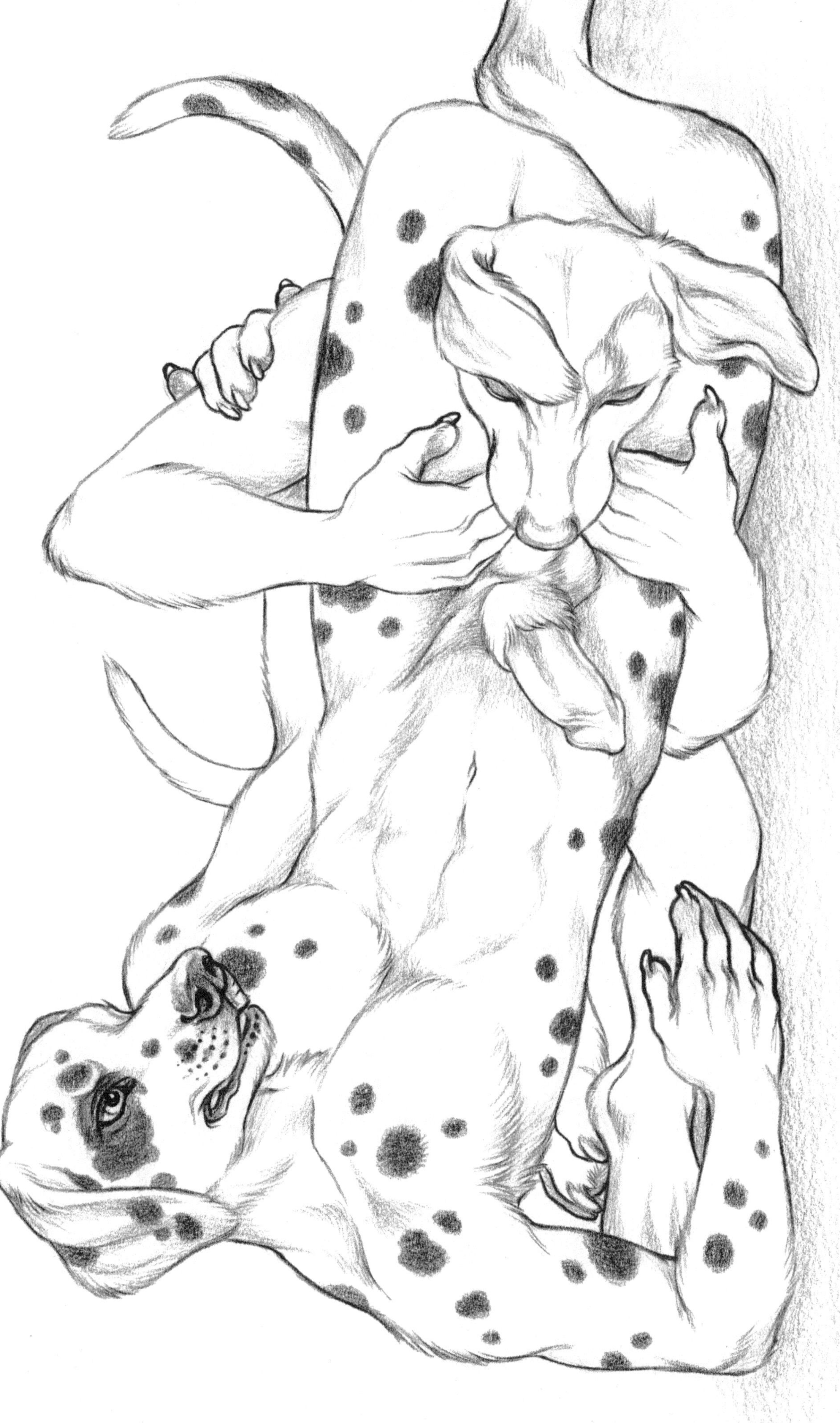